HAPPILY ENEMY AFTER

Hawthorne Brothers Book 2

ASHLEE PRICE

MORE BOOKS FROM ASHLEE PRICE

https://www.ashleepriceromanceauthor.com/

PROLOGUE

Violet

"Isn't Asher Hawthorne hot?"

My friend Casey lets out a dreamy sigh while stirring her iced French vanilla latte.

I know she's younger than me, but I swear she sometimes acts like she's still in high school instead of a twenty-two-year-old trying to get two degrees.

Still, I glance over my shoulder. I immediately spot who Casey is ogling. I've had a few classes with Asher Hawthorne. Even if I hadn't, everyone at UPenn, let alone Wharton, knows who he is. Son of Winston Hawthorne, founder and CEO of Hawthorne Holdings. Why he needs an MBA I don't know. I'm sure he already has a sleek office waiting for him along with a slew of talented professionals whose hard work and ideas he can take credit for.

He's standing next to the counter chatting with another guy while waiting for his order. Dark locks peek from beneath his fitted navy blue beanie. The top button of his charcoal gray Henley shirt is undone, the placket drawing attention to a chiseled chest. Toned biceps threaten to burst through the sleeves that are rolled up to his elbows. The hems of his khakis are rolled just slightly around his ankles, too, giving them a clean look to go with his pristine white sneakers. He knows a thing or two about fashion, I'll give him that.

Just then, he laughs as he takes off his beanie. The sound travels across the room like a deep rumble of thunder that echoes inside my chest. The lines around his mouth crinkle. His ebony eyes dance. The gold bezel of his watch—probably a Chopard or a Piaget—gleams on his wrist as he playfully ruffles his wavy hair.

I look away and douse the admiration welling up in me with a generous sip of steaming hazelnut cappuccino.

Ouch. That's hot.

Fine. Asher Hawthorne is hot as hell. That doesn't mean I'm going to start drooling over him or consider spreading my legs for him like every other female on campus. In fact, I still don't like him.

Casey lets out another sigh, her gaze still pinned beyond my shoulder. "Wouldn't you want to have a piece of him?"

"I would," I answer. "I'd like to cut off his dick."

Casey makes a face. "Gross."

"Then he wouldn't be able to fuck every woman in my class. Or the female professors. Or the research assistants. Or that woman behind the counter preparing his drink."

Casey nods. "She does seem to be drooling over him."

"You mean like you?"

She wipes her mouth with the back of her hand, then with a napkin.

"It's not my fault he looks so delicious. He's like this sugar-coated, cream-filled churro that has the tip dipped in chocolate and you just want to suck the chocolate and lick all the sugar and—"

I put up a hand to silence her. "Now you're being gross."

"And it's not just looks that he has. He's extremely rich."

"Because he was born into a family with lots of money."

It's not like he earned a single cent.

"And he's friendly," Casey says.

"You mean he's cunning. He knows just what to say to people to get what he wants out of them."

"Which just goes to show how smart he is, right? I've heard he can solve differential equations mentally. In less than a minute."

I've heard that, too. I've seen him do equations on the board with just his eyes. I can't deny he's some kind of math whiz. That just annoys me even more. Isn't it enough that he's heir to billions and he looks like Henry Cavill? He has to be a genius, too?

"So what?" I shrug. "He only uses his looks, his money and his brains to get women into his bed. Don't you find that despicable?"

Casey touches her chin. "Well..."

"He already has the world. Why can't he content himself with one woman?"

"Maybe he hasn't found the right one," Casey says. "Maybe he's still searching."

"All of us are searching," I tell her. "But are all of us jumping from one one-night stand to the next? No. And yet that's exactly what he's doing. He isn't trying to see if one of those women is good enough for him. He never intended to keep any of them. They're just things to him, toys to play with and then throw away like the hundreds of toys he probably had growing up. What person who's right in the head does that?"

"Violet."

"I bet he isn't. Right in the head, I mean. Maybe he's treating women like trash because he feels like trash. Maybe his mother didn't love him. Or his father."

"Violet."

"Maybe Asher Hawthorne's just not capable of love." I lean back and fold my arms over my breasts. "Which is pathetic, really. He's just a child. I bet he doesn't know how to—"

I stop talking because I hear a throat clear behind me. I lift my head and find myself staring into a pair of tar-black eyes.

Speaking of the devil. Oh shit.

I quickly turn away and pick up my cup of coffee. It's still hot, but nowhere near as hot as my cheeks, which feel like they're evaporating. I wish I could evaporate and vanish from here.

Violet, you are such an idiot.

"Hi, Asher," Casey greets.

I try to catch her gaze so I can tell her with my eyes to make him go away, but her attention is completely on him. Of course it is.

"Hi."

He offers her his hand and she shakes it while obviously trying to hold back her profuse enthusiasm.

"I don't believe we've met."

"Cassandra," she introduces herself. "But you can call me Casey. Junior. Huntsman Program. Math isn't my favorite subject but I know five languages. And I know how to cook."

I roll my eyes. What's this? A girlfriend résumé? Why doesn't she just ask him outright if he wants to have sex with her? I'm sure he does.

"Huntsman, hmm?" Asher replies. "Impressive."

See.

"And this is Violet Cleary."

I almost choke on my coffee.

"She's pursuing an MBA just like you. She's good at math, too. And she... Ow!"

She pulls her hand away right after I give it a hard squeeze. Then she glares at me.

"What the hell?"

That's my line.

"Well, it's a pleasure to meet both of you," Asher says. "Especially you, Casey. Enjoy your coffee. Maybe next time, you and I can grab a cup."

So he's ignoring me?

Casey gives him a smile. "I'd love that."

"Good."

I hear him start to walk away.

"Oh, and I love your shirt!" Casey calls after him. Then she continues in a softer voice only I can hear. "Though I think you'd look better without it."

I put my cup down and frown. "I swear if you faint, I'm going to leave you here."

She doesn't seem to have heard me. Her gaze is still towards the other end of the room.

"He is so much hotter up close."

"And more arrogant."

I bet he was smirking as he walked away.

"You're just jealous because I'm the one he asked out for a cup of coffee."

I make a sweeping motion with my hands. "By all means, have him. Please."

After all, there's no way I'd ever be interested in going out with Asher Hawthorne.

~

Fine. Maybe I'd be a little interested.

I make the concession as I slowly traverse one of the Classic Literature aisles in the library, my fingertips brushing against the spines of the books.

I'm not a voracious reader, but I did own a copy of Pride and Prejudice once. For a time, I wished I had my own Mr. Darcy to give me a comfortable life.

Now, I'm determined to give that to myself. That's why I studied economics and finance diligently even though what I wanted was to be a math teacher for the fifth or sixth grade, the best years of my life. That's why I'm here at Wharton trying to give myself the best chance of success in the corporate world. Still, sometimes, I can't help but wonder what it would feel like if I didn't have to work, if I could follow my dream, if I didn't have to worry about money because I had a wealthy, supportive husband who could give me just as much as I needed.

A man like Asher Hawthorne.

Whoa. Just a while ago, I was against dating him. Now, I'm thinking of marrying him? No way.

Asher Hawthorne may be wealthy, but he's still a pompous ass. And a playboy. And...

"Looking for something?" A voice interrupts my thoughts.

I turn my head and see Asher standing right in front of me.

Shit.

I hug my laptop to my chest as I step back. My heart pounds against the padded cotton.

How many times does he plan on nearly giving me a heart attack before this day is over?

"Violet, right?" he asks.

Why did Casey have to give him my name?

"Yes," I reply, not feeling like I have any other choice. "If you're looking for Casey, she's—"

"I'm not looking for Casey."

The certainty in his voice matched by the intensity of his gaze—why is he looking at me like

I'm some kind of prey?—sends a shiver down my spine. A lump forms in my throat.

I swallow. "Well, I'm not looking for any book, either, so I'm going."

I turn around and start to walk away.

Why did I have to bump into Asher of all people?

"Wait."

I let out a deep breath as I stop in my tracks. Now what?

"Lloyd Finley is throwing a party at his house tomorrow night. I was wondering if you'd like to go with me."

My eyebrows crease. He's asking me out? Didn't he hear all the things I said about him? Is he just going to ignore all that? Is this some kind of mockery or masochism?

"No, thanks," I give him my straight answer and keep walking.

"Why not?"

Okay. So the rumors are right. This man doesn't take no for an answer.

I draw a deep breath and turn around. "Aren't you a little too old for parties?"

"Aren't you a little too young to be living your life so seriously?" he retorts.

I narrow my eyes at him. "How I live my life is none of your business."

"But my life is yours? What was that you said? That my parents didn't love me?"

So he did hear me at the café. I suddenly feel like I'm back there. My cheeks burn. Still, I hold my chin high and look him in the eye.

"Has anyone ever told you that it's bad to eavesdrop?"

"I overheard. I didn't eavesdrop. There's a difference."

He's being smart with me now? "You didn't overhear. You walked over to our table."

"I walked to the condiment bar. Your table happened to be right next to it."

Come to think of it, Asher's right. The condiment bar was right behind my chair. Still, that doesn't mean it was right for him to listen in to my conversation with Casey.

"So you just decided to drop by and flirt? Is that one of your MOs? Flirting with women while putting some extra sugar in your coffee?"

He scratches his chin. "Wow. You really do hate me, don't you?"

I wrap my hand around my throat and give him a sad look. "Oh, I'm sorry. Did I hurt your nonexistent feelings?"

"Why? What did I ever do to you?"

"Make me think that there really are no decent men left in this world."

"Then let me change your mind," he offers. "Spend some time with me. Get to know the real me."

My eyebrows arch. "The real you?"

"Yes. The me who has a heart."

I snort.

"And if you still think I'm a jerk, then at least you can tell your friends based on firsthand experience instead of relying on just gossip."

Very clever. I almost want to give in. But I don't.

"Nice try, but no. That's spelled N-O. Go ahead and add that to your vocabulary."

I thought that would make Asher frown, but he just grins.

"How about F-U-N? Have you considered adding that to your vocabulary?"

I shake my head. "Wow. I thought you were only good at math, but I guess you can spell, too."

"And I also happen to know how to use a water rower. I noticed you were eyeing the one at the gym. I can teach you how to use it."

My eyes grow wide. Asher saw me at the gym? When?

It sounds creepy. Definitely. At the same time, I can't help but feel a spark of excitement in my chest.

Asher has noticed me before. And he remembers me. As smart as he is, surely he can't remember every woman he sees on campus. But he remembers me.

Then the voice of reason speaks up inside my head. So what? It doesn't mean anything.

"Thanks for the offer, but I'm not looking for a personal trainer."

Of course he'd know how to use a water rower. He probably has his own gym. But I'd rather row a real boat by myself across a lake shrouded in fog than have him standing next to me when I'm just in a tank top, leggings and a layer of sweat.

"Okay, but I'm still looking for someone to go to a party with."

He's persistent. I'll give him that.

"So go look. Elsewhere."

I turn away. I haven't taken a step yet when Asher speaks again.

"You know who Lloyd Finley is, right? His family owns chunks of quite a few banks and insurance companies."

"No wonder you're friends. Your yachts must be anchored at the same marina."

"The CEOs of those banks and insurance companies will be at that party. Along with a few others. I think it would be a good chance for you to learn some things about the world you plan on being a part of, a chance to weigh employment prospects, maybe throw your name out there."

A chance to make all-important connections, which is essentially what business is about. Tempting.

I turn to face him again. "So you're saying you're doing me a favor?"

"I'm saying you'd be doing yourself a favor," Asher answers. "I just want my date."

How generous.

"Frankly, I think I'm the one getting a better bargain," he adds.

Now he's trying to flatter me. Desperate, but cute.

I step forward. "Why me?"

"Because I like how your blue eyes clash with your black hair," Asher confesses. "It reminds me of the ocean at night. Besides, it's a combination I've never seen before."

That's because it's a rare combination, one of the rarest hair and eye color combinations actually. Just as I thought, he just wants to add me to his collection because I'm an unusual find, the same way a boy wants to have a rare Pokémon card in his deck so he can brag about being the only one who has it among his friends.

I'm insulted.

"Also, I was impressed with that report you gave on uncertainty and elasticity of demand," he adds.

Now, I wasn't expecting that. I didn't even know he was listening when I gave that report.

"I think your mind would be an asset to any large company."

My eyes narrow. "Are you trying to recruit me?"

"I might."

"But you want me to meet with people from other companies?"

"What can I say? I'm not afraid of competition."

No, he's not. In fact, I think it thrills him. I guess that's one thing we have in common.

"For now, I'm just asking for one night," Asher says.

And I'm not sure exactly how it happened, but right now, I'm leaning towards saying yes. I don't like Asher. I still feel insulted by what he said earlier and I definitely don't trust him. But I can't deny that this is a good opportunity for me. Too good.

If you want to succeed in the corporate world, you have to look ahead. You also have to get along with people you don't necessarily like. Enduring Asher's company may be a small price to pay for an investment in my future.

"Fine," I give in. "But I'm not counting this as a date."

"I am."

Look at him with that cocky, triumphant grin like he just won the lottery. But this will be my win.

I put up a finger. "On one condition."

"What?"

"We keep this a secret."

I don't want him bragging about our date like some kind of trophy.

"Don't worry," he says. "I never kiss and tell."

Kiss? My gaze falls on Asher's lips and my cheeks grow warm again.

I draw a breath. "There will be no kissing."

"We'll see."

He thinks he can change my mind about that? Fine. I'll let him hope.

"So I'll pick you up in front of the café tomorrow at six-thirty? The party's at seven."

I nod. "Sure."

~

I shouldn't have said yes.

I wrestle with my second thoughts as I fight a losing battle with my stubborn curls in front of the mirror. They've always been stubborn, but I've never minded as much as I do now.

I tug at them with my brush and grit my teeth. "Come on!"

I tell myself I'm doing all this—putting my hair up, wearing my mother's necklace, my best lipstick, my best dress and my least comfortable shoes—because I want to impress the corporate bigshots I'll be shaking hands with. But in truth, I'm doing it for Asher.

It's stupid. I know. This isn't a date. I told Asher so. And I didn't even want to go out with him in the first place. I still haven't changed my mind about him being a jerk. Yet here I am wanting to look pretty for tonight.

No. Not just pretty. Perfect.

I didn't even feel this way for my prom or my first date, which was with a guy named Chuck who I didn't even like all that much.

Oh well. He is Asher Hawthorne, after all. I don't want to be by his side looking like... well, like I shouldn't be by his side. I don't want to embarrass him. I want him to be proud of me.

Yes, he's a playboy. Yes, he's heir to billions. But for just one night, I can think of him as my Mr. Darcy. And I'll be Elizabeth. And maybe, just maybe, we can have a perfect time together at this ball. Party, I mean.

If only I can get my hair into a Victorian-style updo.

I make a few more attempts at it, then throw my brush into the sink and let out a sigh.

"To hell with it."

And if Asher doesn't like how I look, he can go there too.

~

"You look stunning," Asher tells me when the two of us are alone in the gazebo. "I know I told you that earlier, but I just felt like saying it again."

For a moment, I consider telling him that he looks good, too, which he does in his maroon shirt, dark fitted jeans and tan sports blazer. I even think he smells good, the kind of good that makes me want to wrap my arms around him from behind so I can breathe in more of the scent from his nape. Not that I'd ever tell him that.

"Thank you," I say instead while trying not to blush. Then I take another sip of champagne.

Why did I allow Asher to bring me here in the middle of the gardens where there's no one else around? Yes, it's a nice reprieve because it's quiet here. But it's too quiet. And a little dark. Also, kind of romantic with the flowers that are still in bloom swaying in the breeze and the fallen leaves scattered on the lawn looking like specks of gold under the moonlight.

Not a good idea. I must be drunk after having two glasses of champagne. Either that or my mental capacity must have diminished from trying to impress all those pretentious, pompous asses. I can't believe I'm going to have to kiss a few over the next few years.

"I know you said the guest list at this party would be high-profile, but I didn't think it would be that high-profile," I tell Asher.

He gives me a puzzled look. "You mean I didn't tell you that this was a birthday party Lloyd Finley was throwing for his father, Marcus Finley, and that he'd invited all of his former peers and protégés."

"You know you didn't."

"And yet you still handled them all excellently," Asher tells me with another smile that makes my knees weak. "I was right to bring you along."

I take another sip of champagne as I fight off another blush. Why is he being so nice all of a sudden?

No. Not all of a sudden. He's been perfectly nice to me all evening. Nicer than Mr. Darcy. Maybe that's why I had no objections to following him here. Maybe I'm actually hoping he'll kiss me next. He's been so nice to me that I wouldn't mind.

"By the way," Asher says. "You're right."

My eyebrows furrow. "About what?"

"A mother's love is not something I'm overly familiar with. She died when I was ten. And before that, she was sick for a long time. I barely saw her."

Shit. I suddenly feel like punching myself in the gut.

"But I'd like to think that hasn't made me a monster."

I set down my glass. "Of course it hasn't."

He lifts an eyebrow. "Really? But you said—"

"I'm so sorry about what I said," I tell Asher with all the sincerity I can muster. "Especially what I said about your mother. That was a mean and careless remark and I take it back. I'm sorry."

He shakes his head and takes my hand in his. "I forgive you."

I let out a breath of relief.

"At least, I will if you tell me one thing," he says.

"What?"

"You said I affirmed your belief that there were no decent men in the world. Who put that belief in your head? Who broke your heart? First boyfriend?"

"Dad," I answer truthfully. "He broke my mom's heart, and after that everything else just… broke too."

"Oh."

I don't know why I told him that. I've never told anyone about that since high school. Now that he's fallen silent, I regret it. The last thing I want is his pity. I fearfully glance at him, only to find none of that in his eyes.

"You want to know a secret?" he asks.

"What?"

"My dad's not the best either. And I'm definitely not his favorite. Either Ethan or Ryker is. But hey, we can't let our parents' behavior or decisions dictate who we are or how we want to live, right?"

I smile. Now I really want that kiss. In fact, if he doesn't make a move soon, I might just go ahead and give him one.

I turn my body so that I'm right in front of him. Then I stroke his hand.

"So I'm forgiven?"

Asher nods. "Yes."

He places his hand on my cheek and leans forward. I close my eyes. A moment later, his lips press against mine. I kiss him back.

He strokes my cheek and my shoulder as his mouth crushes mine. Heat trickles down my spine and floods my chest. I can't breathe.

He pulls away and I finally get a gulp of air, but my throat tightens as I meet his gaze. Smoldering. Stirring. Excitement simmers in my veins.

He kisses me again. And again. And again. I clutch the front of his jacket and try to keep up, try to breathe in between. He traps my lower lip. My heart skips a beat. Then he wraps an arm around me and pushes his tongue past my lips. When it brushes against my own tongue, my mouth catches fire. My knees tremble.

Each time his tongue rubs against mine, I feel like melting. And I want to. I want Asher to mold my body into a shape meant just for him. I want it to meld with his.

I want him. So much so the desire throbs in my breasts and between my legs. When Asher's hand cups my breast through my dress, I don't protest. When his other hand climbs up my thigh beneath my skirt, I start to give in.

But the voice inside my head shouts.

Stop! Don't do this, Violet! Think.

The moment I start to, the haze in my mind dissipates. The heat beneath my skin evaporates. I realize I don't want this. Not now. Not here. Not like this.

I grab Asher's wrist to stop his hand before his fingers reach my underwear. I pull my mouth away and step back.

Asher looks dismayed, confused. I draw a deep breath.

"We should stop... for now."

For a moment more, his eyebrows remain furrowed. Then he scratches the back of his head and nods.

"Okay."

Is it? He looks agitated, frustrated, defeated. I feel a pang of guilt.

I reach for his hand to extend some comfort but he steps away.

"I think I'll go back to the house," he says.

He's leaving me?

"Asher..."

"I'll get you more champagne." He grabs my nearly empty glass. "And maybe get us some real food from the kitchen. Those hors d'oeuvres barely reached my stomach."

Oh. He just wants some space. That's fine. Hopefully, he can walk off some of his frustration and we can reset the scene when he comes back. This awkward atmosphere will be gone and the two of us can just have a nice conversation like the one we were having before we kissed.

I nod. "Okay."

Asher gives me a smile. "I'll be right back."

~

He's not back yet.

I glance at my watch again. Forty minutes have passed. Forty-two, actually.

I told myself Asher would take just fifteen at most. When he wasn't back by twenty, I wondered if maybe he'd bumped into someone he needed to talk to. After five more minutes, I thought of calling him just to find out what was keeping him—only to realize I didn't have his number. I started to worry. Now that forty-two minutes have passed, I'm thinking either he bumped into several people or he's asking the chef to prepare something from scratch. Or something bad has happened to him and nobody has come to notify me because no one else knows I'm here.

That last thought sends me walking briskly back to the house—as briskly as I can in my two-inch heels—while I rub my arms through my shawl to ward off the chill from the air. As I approach, I hear no commotion, no sirens. The music is still playing. People are still chatting. Champagne and hors d'oeuvres are still being served. I let out a breath of relief.

At least I get the feeling Asher is safe. But I still have to find him.

I search the kitchen first. Asher isn't there and none of the household staff or caterers have seen him. I comb the crowd next. No sign of him either. Where the hell is he? Finally, I decide to ask Lloyd if he knows where Asher is. When he says he doesn't, I ask if I can search the rest of the house. He gives me permission.

I search every room, my heart racing and my thoughts jumbling to come up with explanations for his absence, many of which hurt too much for me to dwell on. I try not to, but when I still don't find Asher after looking everywhere, I start to worry. Where on earth can he be?

Finally, I spot him while I'm standing on the balcony. He's on the front steps. I'm about to call his name, but then I notice there's a woman standing next to him. Tall. Brunette. Glistening red dress. Diamonds around her neck. Arm around Asher's waist.

His Maserati Levante stops right in front of them and the valet gets out. As Asher goes around the front of the vehicle to take the driver's seat, the butler opens the door to the passenger side and the woman slips in. Asher gets in the car and it heads down the private road leading out of the property, the same road we took coming in. Within seconds, the vehicle disappears from sight.

For a while, I just stand there on the balcony gripping the railing, frozen and numb. The scene I just saw of Asher leaving with another woman plays over and over inside my head until it finally sinks in.

Asher left the party. With another woman. Even though he came to the party with me. Even though he asked me to come to this party with him. Even though he kissed me and said he'd come back to me.

My chest constricts. My heart feels like it's being crushed. I want to scream. I want to cry. I want to jump from this balcony. Instead, I go inside. I lean against a wall and slap my forehead.

Stupid Violet! Did you really think he cared about you? Because he asked you out? Because he was nice to you? Because he kissed you? Did you really think he would come back after you rejected him? Of course he wasn't going to. Sex was all he was after, and since you rejected him, he had no reason to hang out with you.

Unbelievable. But at the same time, I should have expected it. I should have known sex was all Asher was after. I should have known he'd discard me as soon as he realized he had no use for me. I should have known he wouldn't even have the decency to drive me home.

I should have known Asher Hawthorne would break my heart.

No. I knew it was a possibility, but I went out with him anyway. I allowed myself to be swayed by his sweet words anyway. I opened up to him anyway. I kissed him anyway.

And now, here I am in this pretty dress, my cheeks cold, my feet sore and my heart torn to pieces.

This is what I get for daring to dream.

But I know better now. Even though I feel like breaking down, I hold my shoulders square. Even as I shatter, I'm turning my resolve into steel.

I'm going to forget all about Asher Hawthorne, and I'm never going to let any man make a fool of me again, no matter how handsome or wealthy or clever he is.

Never again.

CHAPTER ONE

Asher

Five years later...

So we meet again.

I stare at Violet Cleary as she stands on the descending escalator in a yellow ombre dress that seems to wrap around her like a flame. Most of her black curls are gathered at the top of her head but some still cascade past her ears down to her shoulders.

I remember a woman with black curls that I dated once. Just once. She had the most beautiful blue eyes, too. Too bad I can't remember her name—I'm terrible with names—and too bad I never got to sleep with her.

I set the memory of her aside as I prepare to greet Violet. No use dwelling on the past. I have to focus on the present, on this amazing woman I met in Switzerland who's going to be working with me starting tomorrow.

I know what my brothers think—Asher's going after another woman again. They think I do this just for fun. Well, it is fun. Usually. This time, it's different. Ever since I met Violet, I just knew I had to have her. I've been with a lot of women, but I've never wanted a woman this much. And not just in my bed. I want to make her fall for me. I want her to drop her guard, to wipe that serious, snobbish expression off her face. Something tells me both are just masks, barbed wire on the fence to keep people out. I want to see the real her, to know the real her. The fact that she's been thwarting all my efforts to get close to her so far has only made me want her more.

One way or another, I am going to get what I want.

I walk towards her after she gets off the escalator.

"Welcome to Chicago, Violet. I trust your flight was comfortable? We did put you in first class."

Her brown eyes narrow. "What are you doing here, Mr. Hawthorne?"

In other words, she's not happy to see me. Well, I had a feeling she wouldn't be, but I'm still here.

"Asher, please," I tell her. "There are three Mr. Hawthornes in the company, so it's best if you call me Asher."

"Or maybe I'll just call the CEO Ethan and your younger brother Ryker and I'll call you Mr. Hawthorne."

I let out a breath. And here I thought coming to America would make her a little less… cold. But I guess she's just like the Swiss Alps—covered in snow all year long. Well, in that case, I'll just have to turn on the heat and be global warming.

I keep my smile on. "To answer your question, I'm here to give you a warm welcome to our fair, windy city and also to give you a ride to the office."

"Wow." She puts a hand on her hip. "I didn't realize one of the duties of a CFO was picking up employees from the airport."

"Not all employees," I say. "Just the most talented one from this Zurich-based company which happens to be the newest and most promising addition to Hawthorne Holdings."

Violet rolls her eyes. "Flattery will get you nowhere, Mr. Hawthorne. Surely I taught you that in Zurich?"

"It's not flattery if it's the truth."

"It is flattery if your intention is to make me like you, which I can assure you will not happen, so you're only wasting your time."

"But I'll be your boss. Weren't you informed?"

"I was," she answers with an expression that tells me she doesn't like it one bit. "But I wasn't aware I was required to like my boss. I definitely didn't read anything like that in my contract."

Stubborn. But somehow, that's one of the things I happen to like about her.

I'll make her like me. Eventually. For now, I'll just get her out of this airport.

"How many suitcases do you have?" I ask her.

She glances at the red one next to her. "Just this one."

"You don't look like you have enough shoes in there," I joke.

Violet doesn't laugh. "You want to know what's in my suitcase?"

I admit I'm curious. "What?"

She leans towards me to whisper in my ear. "The dead body of the asshole who tried to undress me with his eyes inside the plane. Think you know a place where I can dump it?"

I look at her. I know she's joking, but I also know she's trying to warn me. Ha. She thinks she can scare me off that easily? Not a chance.

I grab her suitcase. "Actually, I do. And I'm glad you took care of him, though in the future, you won't have to. As long as you're with me, I'll take care of any assholes who dare to come near you."

She gives me a sarcastic smile. "How noble."

"Yup. I'm your knight in shining armor." I glance at the exit. "So shall we go to your carriage, milady?"

~

"This isn't the office," Violet complains after we get out of the car in front of a restaurant.

"No," I tell her. "This is one of the best restaurants in Chicago."

"And we're here because?"

"We're having our first meeting over lunch, which also doubles as your welcome party."

She pauses. "But I thought I wasn't starting until tomorrow."

I hear the worry in her voice so I turn to her with a grin.

"Don't worry. It will just be a short meeting."

She touches her hair and the front of her dress. "But I... I'm not dressed for... work. I haven't changed yet. I..."

So Violet can get flustered, too, can she? It's a refreshing change, but I decide not to torture her any longer.

"I'm just kidding. We're just here to eat."

She pouts and glares at me.

I shrug. "I thought you might want to have something to eat now that you're on the ground. I know you were in first class but I, for one, can't eat any airplane food. Did you?"

"I ate a little," she answers, her voice back to being cold.

"Then you must be hungry. I know I am."

I walk up the steps to the restaurant and the maître d' opens the door.

"Welcome, Mr. Hawthorne. I have your table ready."

I acknowledge him with a smile before following him.

"Wait," Violet says. "I'm not hungry. I'll just wait in the car."

"Nonsense. You're staying here with me. You don't have to eat much. Just have something. Anything. Everything on the menu here is delicious."

"But—"

"It's just lunch, Violet," I cut her off as I face her. "And the company's paying."

"That's not what I'm worried about."

"No. You're worried I might try to seduce you, especially since there don't seem to be any other customers around. I can explain. This restaurant usually doesn't open until five, but for us, they've made an exception. It's not the first time. Also, I can assure you that I'll be on my best behavior."

Violet doesn't look convinced, so I put my hands up.

"I promise I won't flirt. Like I said, it's just lunch. And no, it's not a date. Just two people eating good food."

She sighs but doesn't raise any more concerns.

"Good."

I walk to the table. She follows silently. We place our orders—mushrooms, lamb and a glass of wine for me, salad and a cup of coffee for her. As we wait for them to arrive, Violet takes out her phone and focuses her attention on it in a clear effort to avoid talking to me or even looking at me.

I don't know why she hates me so much. It's like she took one look at me and slammed the door in my face. It's unlike anything I've ever experienced before.

Well, that woman with the black curls did slam the door in my face, too. And with her, I never got another chance—but with Violet, I'll have plenty. Now that we're going to be in the same country, in the same building, on the same floor, she won't be able to run away or hide from me. I just have to keep knocking on her door.

"Do you miss Switzerland already?" I ask her as I pick up my glass of wine.

"A little," Violet answers without looking up from her phone.

"What do you think you'll miss the most about it?"

"The fact that people there mind their own business."

In other words, she wants me to shut up. But I'm not going to. I don't get what I want, she doesn't get what she wants.

"Have you lived there all your life? Are your parents Swiss?"

She narrows her eyes at me.

"What?" I ask her.

"My God, you really don't have a clue, do you?"

I'm still confused. "I don't know what you're talking about."

For a moment, Violet falls silent. Then, to my surprise, she bursts out laughing.

I'm glad I finally heard her laugh. I want to laugh with her. But something tells me the joke's on me.

"I'm sorry, but what's funny, exactly?"

"You," she answers after she calms down and takes a sip of her coffee. "But not in a good way."

I shake my head. "I still don't get it."

She grins. "Nothing new."

What does that mean? Does it mean we've met before? When? Where?

"I don't understand," I tell her.

"And you never will," she replies.

Just then, the waiter arrives with my mushrooms and her salad. Violet places her napkin on her lap and picks up her fork. I'm still at a loss.

"I thought we were here to eat," Violet says before stuffing some greens inside her mouth. "Mm. You're right. The food here is good."

Finally, something out of her mouth that I can comprehend. And that isn't an insult.

I grab my napkin and my utensils. I still don't know what Violet was talking about earlier, and that infuriates me, but for now I guess I'll just enjoy eating with her.

"I thought you weren't hungry," I remark before eating a mushroom.

"I guess I am," she confesses. "Maybe it's because I'm in a better mood now."

At my expense. But if that's the price of her company, then fine. I'll shoulder it this time.

"Just eat. You're going to need a good amount of energy for the VIP tour of HQ I'm going to give you."

~

"And here we are, back at your office," I say at the end of the tour. "I hope you liked everything you saw."

"I think I did," Violet tells me. "And I learned a lot, apart from the fact that the CFO apparently has too much time on his hands."

I grin. "Don't worry. I'll catch up on work tomorrow, especially with your help."

She lets out a breath. "I was afraid of that."

"Just kidding. I already finished my work for the day this morning. So…" I sit on the edge of her desk and rub my hands together. "Any final questions? Anything you want changed in your office?"

"I'd love it if it was a bit farther from yours," she answers.

I shake my head. "Nope. I'm afraid this is the only office we can spare on this part of the floor."

"Of course." She steps forward. "What about not having you sitting on my desk? Think that's too much to ask?"

"No." I get off her desk.

"Thanks. It looks much better now."

She sits behind her desk.

"You look better behind your desk," I tell her. "Like a boss."

She does. Back at the restaurant, she changed into a black dress, so she looks more professional now. I saw how she commanded respect during the tour. I even saw a few jaws drop. I can already tell that things are going to be more interesting around here with her around.

"Maybe I'll take your job someday," Violet says.

The look on her face tells me she's serious, but I chuckle.

"Nice try. But nope. Not happening."

"Because you're the CEO's little brother?"

"Because I'm very good at what I do."

"Better than me?"

"Yes."

"We'll see." She taps her fingers on the table. "I'd be more careful from now on if I were you, Mr. Hawthorne."

A declaration of war. Is that what all this is about? Her wanting my job? No. I can sense this is all too personal. Plus I can't just forget about that comment she made earlier.

"Tell me why," I demand.

Enough with the clues and the guessing games.

Violet leans back in her chair. "Why what?"

"Why do you see me as a bug that needs to be squished?"

"I don't squish bugs," she says. "I'm not afraid of bugs."

"But you're afraid of me."

"I'm not afraid of you."

"You just find me disgusting?"

"Pretty much."

"Because?"

She draws a deep breath but doesn't give me an answer.

I put my hands on her desk. "I need a reason, Violet. I'm not going to force you to like me or get along with me, but if you're going to fight me at every turn, I at least need to know why."

Violet nods. "Fine. I think I've had enough fun anyway."

Fun?

"Give me a minute," she says. "Oh, and it's best if you turn around."

My eyebrows crease. Turn around? Do I have to?

I realize I do once she starts to take off her contact lens. I turn away immediately. I'm not the least bit squeamish, but I swear I'll never understand how people can stand to put plastic in their eyes.

"Done," Violet says several seconds later. "You can turn around now."

As soon as I do, our gazes meet. My eyes grow wide as I see the color of hers.

Blue. Like sapphires.

"Is that your natural eye color?"

"Yes," she answers. "I have blue eyes and black, curly hair. Believe me, I tried to change that, too, but my hair is just stubborn and the dye irritates my scalp. Anyway, yeah, blue eyes, black hair. Rare combination. Does that ring a bell?"

Fuck.

Violet grins. "Based on that horrified look on your face, I'm guessing it does."

I point a finger at her. "You're that woman."

"You have to be more specific given your record of sleeping around."

"You're the woman from Wharton."

"Still too vague."

"The one I asked out to Lloyd Finley's party."

"Bingo," Violet says. "Now, fast forward to the night of that party, somewhere around nine o'clock, and you'll understand why I want your heart on a platter. Maybe your cock, too."

Now, I remember.

"We kissed in the gazebo."

"Fast forward some more."

I try to recall what happened after that. "I went back into the house. I talked to some people. I can't remember who anymore."

"Then allow me to help you. There was a woman. She was tall. Maybe five ten. Brunette. She was wearing a sparkly red dress."

I remember her. "Kim Anderson. She was a swimmer. I was a fan."

"Obviously."

"She came up to me and—"

Violet puts her hand up. "I don't need to hear the details. The point is you left the party with her even though you arrived with me. I had to call an Uber to get home."

I see. Now it all makes sense. Violet hates me because five years ago when I was at Wharton—

which feels like ancient history now—I took her to a party and I left her there.

Do I have an excuse? No. I was frustrated with her because she was being a cocktease. I had a case of blue balls. Then I met Kim. She was nice. She was willing. I took her back to my apartment. End of story.

Did I feel even a twinge of guilt for leaving Violet? I did. I tried to talk to her after one of our classes, but she avoided me. Then I saw her with some guy and I just assumed she'd moved on, and I did, too. It turns out she never did.

"I'm sorry," I tell her. "But that was ages ago. We were students."

"Grad students. We weren't teenagers, so you can't blame hormones for your behavior."

"But we're professionals now."

"Apparently, that doesn't stop some people from sleeping around."

I roll my eyes.

"You haven't changed," Violet says. "I saw how the women in this place look at you."

"That's my fault?"

"They wouldn't look at you like that, with that hunger and that hope, unless they had some kind of encouragement. You still sleep with one woman after another and then throw them away the morning after, don't you?"

"Not as much as I used to."

Violet laughs. "Like just three women per week?"

I don't answer. "If you go out with me, I won't sleep with anyone else. I promise."

She shakes her head. "Nope. Not falling for that again."

I sigh. "Violet, that was years ago. Can't we just forget about it and start over?"

"No," she answers firmly.

"I already said I was sorry. What do you want me to do? Kneel? Give you a foot massage? Buy you flowers? Whisk you off to the beach and write 'I'm sorry' a hundred times in the sand?"

"Wow." She sits up and clasps her hands on her desk. "Maybe you should quit being CFO and write a book called 101 Ways to Apologize. I bet it would be a hit."

"Do you want me to give you my job? Is that it?"

Her expression turns serious. "No. I don't want you to give me your job, Mr. Hawthorne. I'll take it myself. In fact, I don't want anything from you."

"So you're just going to keep hating me for the rest of your life? Is that it?"

"No," Violet answers. "That would be too exhausting. I already stopped hating you once, you know. When I was in Switzerland, I forgot about you. But you showed up and here I am hating you again. But I'll stop eventually. I'll go back to just pretending you don't exist, to not feeling anything at all for you."

"So you admit you still have feelings for me?"

"Hate. Disgust. All that ugly stuff."

"Damaging stuff," I say. "Why not just let them go and give me a second chance?"

Violet puts her hand on her chest as she snickers. "A second chance?"

I shrug. "Why not? Everyone deserves a second chance."

"Bullshit." Violet stands up and narrows her eyes at me. "If you think I'm going to give you another chance to make me feel like a fool and a piece of trash, you're dead wrong."

"I'm not going to do that."

"No. You're not. End of conversation."

Violet sits down. I draw a deep breath.

"Can't we at least be friends?" I ask her. "We are going to be working together."

"Which is something I never asked for. Do you think I want to work with you? But like you said, we're adults and professionals, so yeah, I'm going to do my job and I'm going to do my best. And one day, I'm going to be CFO. It's that simple."

I scratch the back of my head. Really? She thinks all this is simple?

"I..."

Just then, I hear a knock on the glass door. I turn my head and see Stella stepping in. She stops as our gazes meet.

"Oh, I'm sorry, Asher. I didn't know..."

"Can I help you?" Violet asks.

Stella looks at her. "You must be Violet Cleary. I'm Stella Quinn. We met in Zurich."

"We did?" Violet asks as they shake hands.

"Right. You probably don't remember me because I was in the background. I'm Ethan's... Mr. Hawthorne's assistant."

"Oh."

"He asked me to show you your apartment, so when you're done here, you can—"

"Oh, I'm done here." Violet stands up and looks at me. "We are done here, aren't we, Mr. Hawthorne? Or is there something else I need to make clear?"

"No," I answer. "You were very clear."

"Good."

She grabs her purse and leaves the office with Stella. After they're gone, I sink into Violet's chair. My gaze goes to the freshly engraved name plate on her desk.

Violet Cleary. Controller.

Who would have thought she was the same woman I left at a party years ago?

I'd go back and change that if I could, but I can't. And she won't give me a second chance. So what am I supposed to do? Just sit and smile while she glares at me every single day, spits venom at me every chance she gets, and plots to take my job?

No way. If I'm not going to have my fun, I'm not going to let her have hers. If she won't play nice, then she has no place on the court, on my court. If I can't have her, then she might as well get out of my sight.

Violet brought up a lot of things from the past, but she forgot something important about the present—I'm her boss. I can fire her. I won't, because that's no fun. But I will make her life such a hell that she'll pack her bags and head back to Switzerland.

I gave her a chance to be a saint. She decided to be the devil. So fine. Let's do this. Let's give each other hell and see who has the last laugh.

I pick up the Baoding balls on her desk and rotate them in my hand.

Now, this could be even more fun.

CHAPTER TWO

Violet

"Having fun yet?" Stella asks me after we step inside one of the elevators of The Mistral.

It's a thirty-six story building just ten minutes away from the office. It has a doorman, a security guard, a pair of polite receptionists and a spacious lobby with minimalist furniture, a huge chandelier, mirrors and a succulent garden. I like it already.

But that's not what Stella's asking.

Fun? Let me think. What have I done so far? I had lunch with Asher. The food was good but the company wasn't, so no, that wasn't fun. Although I did enjoy that stupid look on Asher's face when he was struggling to decipher my words. At least, I would have if I wasn't so annoyed that he didn't recognize my name or my face just because I was wearing a pair of contacts. Jerk.

Then I had a tour of the office building. Everything looked fine. The people were warm. But I was also with Asher, who was clearly well-liked, especially by the women, so that wasn't fun either.

That conversation I had with Asher at the end? Maybe, because I was in control, but it was also a bit excruciating to relive that horrible night.

So let's see. My answer is…

"Too much fun, which is why I'm looking forward to slipping under the covers. After a shower, of course."

I can't believe it's been sixteen hours since I had one.

Stella turns to me with a smile. "Don't worry. Your apartment definitely has a shower. And it's fully furnished with fresh linens and rugs and curtains. In fact, everything in it is new. It's a gift from Eth—I mean Mr. Ethan Hawthorne, the CEO."

I wonder why she keeps doing that. I don't really mind her calling the CEO by his first name. I used to call Simone by his first name.

Wait. Did she say my apartment is a gift from the CEO? It's free?

"I'm sorry, but I didn't quite catch the meaning of that. Are you saying I don't have to pay any rent?"

"Oh, no. You do," Stella answers. "I meant the furniture and the appliances and all the trappings, those are Mr. Hawthorne's welcome gift. Mr. Ethan

Hawthorne, that is. But you still have to pay rent. Don't worry, though, because Hawthorne Holdings owns this building, so you get a huge employee discount."

"I see."

I figured a free apartment was too good to be true. But hey, at least I get a discount. Hopefully, it's at least twenty-five percent.

"You can make arrangements downstairs if you want to have your rent deducted straight from your salary," Stella adds.

I nod. "I'll think about that."

The doors open and we get out on the thirty-fourth floor. I find myself at the start of a long carpeted hallway. I only see two doors, though, one at the end and another just a few feet away from me.

"The units in this building are spacious with high ceilings," Stella explains. "So there's a maximum of seven units per floor. But on the thirty-third and this floor, there are only two units."

Okay.

She unlocks the door near me and pushes it open. "And this is yours."

I step inside. As soon as I see the space, I gasp. Spacious? This place is bigger than any apartment I've lived in. It may even be bigger than the whole first floor of the house where I grew up. And the furniture is lovely. Modern but cozy. The design has a feminine touch—warm, soothing pastel colors and a few pieces of floral decor. The view of the city from the floor-to-ceiling windows is spectacular.

I wrap my hand around my throat as I take in the view. The sun is setting so the building facades are gleaming golden. In the distance, the surface of Lake Michigan glistens as it captures the final remnants of daylight.

"I know it's not Zurich, but Chicago has its own charm," Stella says as she stands beside me.

"It sure does," I agree.

She looks around. "So do you like the apartment?"

"I do," I admit as I turn around. "It's… amazing."

"I'm glad you think so. I chose some of the pieces myself. I've been dabbling in interior design lately."

"Really?"

That would explain the feminine touch.

"I'm setting up a nursery soon."

"A nursery?" My eyebrows furrow, but as soon as I see Stella's hand on her belly, I understand. "You're pregnant?"

"Yes. I'm not that far along, so it's not obvious yet, and maybe it is too early for me to be thinking about nurseries. I mean, we don't even know if we're having a boy or a girl. But I just can't help but be excited. Well, I wasn't excited at first. I was really scared, actually. But now I am."

And it shows.

"It's fine," I tell her as I give her hand a squeeze. "Congratulations."

"Thanks."

"And please tell Mr. Hawthorne, Mr. Ethan Hawthorne that is, that I graciously accept his gift and am very grateful."

Stella nods. "I will."

"I'd thank him myself, but I don't want to take up any of his time. I know he's very busy."

"He is, but you can just thank him the first chance you get, like when you bump into him in the corridor or happen to share an elevator ride with him."

I give Stella a puzzled look. "I would have thought he had his own private elevator."

"He does, but every now and then he takes the other one just to let himself be seen, remind his employees that they're all working towards the same goals."

"Really? He didn't strike me as someone who cared about his employees when I met him in Zurich."

Stella grins. "That's because he looks so serious most of the time. Scary even. But he does care. He's actually a big kid at heart."

Her words—and more particularly the tone of her voice—give me pause. There's also that look on her face when she's talking about Ethan Hawthorne. Is this how an assistant talks about her boss? My female intuition tells me no.

Is Stella Ethan Hawthorne's girlfriend? She doesn't seem to be wearing a ring, so she's not his wife or fiancée, and yet there's something there. But she's pregnant. Is it Ethan's? Is that even allowed?

I suddenly have a lot of questions, but I decide to keep my mouth shut. I'm new. I'm curious, but I don't want to be nosy. Besides, who the CEO knocks up, whether it's his assistant or some foreign-born heiress, is really none of my business. I'll give this the Swiss treatment and leave it alone.

Just then, Stella's phone beeps. She looks at it.

"Oops. I have to go. If there's anything wrong with the apartment, you can just call downstairs."

"Okay."

She places her hand on my arm and gives me a warm smile. "Again, welcome to Hawthorne Holdings. Welcome to Chicago. And I wish you all the best."

I pat her hand. "Thank you."

She walks towards the door but stops right in front of it and turns.

"Oh, and one more thing."

"Yes?"

"I know Asher can come on a little too strong sometimes. He can seem careless, thoughtless. Sometimes, it seems like he speaks before he thinks…"

She sounds like she knows Asher well, too. Wait. Don't tell me the baby is Asher's?

"But he actually weighs everything carefully. He may seem lazy, but he takes work very seriously.

And yes, he loves to flirt, but I think he's actually maybe desperately searching for someone who can understand him and challenge him at the same time."

I narrow my eyes at her. I know I said I'd keep my mouth shut, but I just can't rein in my curiosity.

"I'm sorry, but are you and Asher…?"

Stella's eyebrows go up. "What? No!"

She shakes her head.

"So you didn't sleep with Asher?"

"Never."

"So the baby isn't…?"

"Not Asher's," Stella assures me. "Definitely not."

And I believe her. Something in her eyes tells me she's never even been interested in Asher, which is a first, I think, but understandable if she's always been in love with someone else—like Ethan Hawthorne, for example. In fact, I'm even more convinced now that that's the case.

"I'm sorry," I tell her. "It's just… I've heard things about Asher."

Stella nods. "I know. That's why I told you all that stuff just now. Some of the things you heard may have a grain of truth in them, but trust me, Asher isn't a bad guy."

But he is. After all, no decent man goes to a party with one woman, the one he asked and practically begged to go out with him, kisses her and then leaves with another, right?

But I don't say that.

"Thanks," I simply tell Stella.

She gives me another nod and then leaves. I sit on the couch, on the exquisitely soft microfiber couch that still smells new and faces the window, and I let out a deep breath.

So this is my new home, huh?

I wasn't lying when I said I like it. I like Chicago, too. The only thing I don't like about this new job? Asher. He's a textbook jerk. Selfish. Conceited. Obnoxious. He thinks he's God's gift to women, while in truth, he's a curse. He shouldn't exist.

And yet, Stella, who I happen to like, seems to think he's a good guy. She was practically selling him to me, trying to tell me to give him another chance. And the thing is she knows Asher. If she's with Ethan, Asher must be like a brother to her.

That may make her biased, but it also means she knows him well.

What about me? How well do I really know Asher?

I went to school with him, but we barely talked outside of our classes. I only had that one conversation with him before we started kissing and things fell apart. Ever since then, I've thought of him as a monster.

But is he one? I'm judging him based on one fact, one incident, one mistake which he already apologized for. Is that fair? What if I'm wrong about him? What if I'm being too harsh, too rash?

The more I think about it, the more I realize that I don't actually hate him. I just hate what he did. Just that one thing. And I'm to blame for it, too.

Is there a chance that maybe, just maybe, I've been wrong all this time and Asher isn't as bad as I think he is?

~

I'm right. Asher's bad. The worst, actually.

During my first day at the office, Asher dumped a whole pile of work on me. And he keeps adding to it every day. I've barely been able to leave my desk. I've even had to work overtime. On my first week. And if I make so much as a single error, even if it's a typo, or forget one little detail, he's on my case, turning it into a big deal. If I try to say anything in my defense, he glares and tells me that if I can't do my job, I should just quit.

There's no way I'm going to quit, but I don't like this. Not one bit. I'm definitely being punished. And I know it's for personal reasons.

Is it because I threatened to take his job? Or is it because I said I'd never forgive him? Whatever the reason, I think he's being unfair. And he's even worse during meetings.

At the first one, he tried everything he could to make me feel like I didn't belong. Not in that meeting. Not in his department. Not in the company. He made it clear he didn't like me, so now, no one on the floor does. He didn't give me a chance to speak. Each time I started talking, he'd interrupt or move on. And he deliberately talked a lot about things they did in the past that I clearly wasn't a part of and have no knowledge of. It was as if I wasn't there.

I thought the second meeting would be better because he gave me a chance to report, but then afterwards, he started criticizing me, pointing out every mistake I made and telling me I could have done everything better because he could have done it all better. In front of everyone. Even when I was in school, I was never criticized in front of the whole class. It made me want to cry.

And just when I thought it couldn't get any worse, today, at the meeting just now, Asher stole my ideas, all my hard work, all the plans I drew up, the charts, the tables, and passed them off as his. I was so shocked and disappointed I couldn't say anything even if I'd wanted to.

But I can speak now. Enough is enough.

"Mr. Hawthorne?" I get up from my chair as Asher starts to leave the conference room. "A moment, please?"

He keeps going. "I'm busy."

Oh no. He's not running away.

"Asher!" I slam my hands on the table.

That gets his attention. He stops and turns towards me.

"What?"

"This has to stop," I tell him in a calmer tone.

His dark eyes narrow. "I have no idea what you're talking about."

"Yes, you do. Ever since I started working here, you've been dumping work on me. Not just my work but yours. And you've seized every chance to make fun of me, humiliate me and make me feel like I don't belong here."

"How you feel is completely under your control, not mine. So if you feel like you don't belong here, maybe it's because that's what you believe."

"Bullshit. You've been treating me like an outsider, like an amateur, like crap, like—"

"A bug that needs to be squished?" he finishes the sentence. "Or is that too harsh?"

I frown. I knew it. This is personal.

"I'm going to report you to HR," I tell him.

Asher doesn't look the least bit perturbed.

"Say hi to Gina for me, will you? She's the woman in her fifties with the red hair, eyeglasses with cords and the crazy earrings. Looks like your stereotypical librarian. But don't get fooled. She's very good with computers. And very sweet."

My eyebrows furrow. Why is he telling me this?

"Oh, and while you're there, why don't you hand in your resignation?"

"What?"

"You're clearly stressed, overwhelmed even, by your job. Like I said, if you can't handle it, you can just quit. I think you should."

I glare at him. "It's not my job that stresses or overwhelms me, and you know it. You're the one who's making everything difficult for me."

He grins. "I'm the boss. It's my job to make things difficult for everyone."

"I don't see you yelling at anyone else about how to do their jobs."

"That doesn't mean I don't or didn't. Maybe this is just how I treat anyone who's new to my department. An initiation. A baptism of fire, so to speak."

I shake my head. "I don't think so. This is personal and you know it, Asher."

"I believe you're supposed to call me Mr. Hawthorne," he says. "And no. It's not personal, Ms. Cleary. Is it?"

"You know it is," I answer through gritted teeth.

There's no way he can convince me it isn't.

Asher taps his fingers on the table. "You think I'm doing all this to punish you for something you did in the past? I would never do that, Ms. Cleary. I would never let something that happened in the past mess up the present. Or the future."

And yet he's doing exactly that.

"I haven't done anything wrong. You were the one who left me at that party. No. You left me in a gazebo. I could have frozen to death."

"And I said sorry."

"Which you didn't mean."

"I did mean it," he argues. "You just didn't want to accept it."

"So you're punishing me? I refused to forgive you, which isn't a crime. In fact, it's my prerogative. You're the one who can't accept that. You can't even respect it. Instead, you decided to make my life here at work hell."

I scratch my head. Can't Asher see how stupid that sounds?

He crosses his arms over his chest. "Like I said, I'm not punishing you, Ms. Cleary. But if you feel like you're being punished, if you personally feel like you can't get along with me, if you feel like you can't take all this anymore, you're free to go."

Why does he keep saying that? I don't want to quit. If I quit, I lose everything. He wins.

"I'm not going anywhere!"

"Right. Because you want to be CFO eventually."

I draw a breath to calm myself down. "Is that a crime? So you're punishing me for that, too?"

"If that's the case, Ms. Cleary, then I suggest you stick to getting your job done. Perfectly. As long as you do, I will have no complaints."

Yeah, right.

"I might even be convinced to give you a reward. See. I'm an excellent boss. You should be glad to be working under me."

He gives me a final grin that makes my stomach churn and my hands clench into fists. Then he leaves. As soon as he's gone, I grab my pen and throw it at the door. Then I sink into my chair and grip my hair in frustration.

That... that... fucking jerk! I don't know why Stella said he's a good person, but I definitely don't see it. He's a scumbag. He's a monster. He's the devil.

Du lusche! Du hurensohn!

I should never have come here to work for him.

I let out a deep breath and bury my face in my arms on top of the desk.

This is the worst.

CHAPTER THREE

Asher

"This is the best martini you've made so far, Glenn," I praise the bartender after gulping down the last of the gin and dry vermouth in my glass.

Then I grab the toothpick and let both of the olives slide into my mouth.

"And these olives are just divine. Are you getting them somewhere new?"

"From a jar with a different name on it," Glenn answers.

I chuckle and turn to Ryker, my younger brother, who's seated beside me. "Did you know our bartender was so funny?"

"Well, he does need to shake things up every now and then," Ryker answers before taking a sip of his gin tonic.

"Haha. You're funny, too."

He narrows his eyes at me. "You only noticed that now?"

"Well, you always seem so serious."

"No, not always. I just have to act like the adult when I'm around you."

I laugh and signal to Glenn to make me another martini. He nods.

"You seem to be in a good mood," Ryker remarks.

"I am," I admit.

"Things have been going well at work?"

"You can say that."

Who would have thought that giving Violet hell would be just as fun as trying to seduce her?

Well, it hasn't been all fun. There were times I felt like I was the one being punished, times when the guilt was so bad it made my stomach hurt. Whenever I saw her on the verge of tears, I wanted to punch myself. If she had cried right in front of me, I probably would have wrapped my arms around her. And earlier in the conference room, it took everything I had to be mean to her and walk away when all I wanted was to have sex with her on top of that conference table. Hot, angry sex. The best kind.

Still, I think it's only a matter of time before that happens. Or she quits. Either way, I win. So yeah, I guess things have been going well at work.

I take a sip from my fresh martini. "What about you? How are things at work?"

I know we both work in the same building, but we're on different floors, in different departments—me in Finance, Ryker in Acquisitions. We might as well be living on different planets.

"Good," he answers. "Things are starting to settle down. I don't think the company is making any other acquisitions for the rest of the year."

After all the trouble we all went through to get Odermatt Inc., I didn't think so either.

"Which means you can take things easy for a while," I tell him. "Good for you."

We raise our glasses and let them clink before sipping our respective drinks. As I put my glass down, I see the empty seat next to me and glance at the door to the bar.

"Where's Ethan, by the way? Is he coming?"

"I thought he sent you a message, too."

I check my phone. "No. What did he say?"

"That he can't make it."

"Because?"

"Guess."

I only have one in mind. "He's with Stella?"

Ryker grins. "Bull's-eye."

Of course he is. These Friday midnight drinking sessions are supposed to be our time together as brothers, but ever since Ethan found out Stella is pregnant, the stool beside me has been empty more often than not. After Stella gives birth, he might stop coming altogether.

And I understand. He's starting a family of his own now. I know. I just wish he didn't leave me and Ryker behind.

"It's unfair," I say. "We promised we'd meet each other for drinks every Friday no matter what."

"And we've been doing it for years," Ryker says. "But we can't do it forever."

"Said who?"

"Ethan is going to be a father soon. He's going to have a family of his own. Of course he's going to be spending as much time as he can with them."

"That doesn't mean he can't hang out with us anymore. We're still his brothers."

"And as his brothers, we'll always be there to support him when he needs us, regardless of whether or not he goes drinking with us."

I snort. "You're too nice, Ryker. Do you know that?"

"And you're just jealous," he points out.

"Of Stella because Ethan is spending more time with her?"

That sounds stupid.

"Of Ethan because he has Stella," Ryker answers.

I fall silent. Am I?

I know the gears in my head have been turning. Ever since Ethan, who I never thought would take romance seriously or fall in love, got together with Stella, I've been wondering if the same thing can happen to me. Seeing them so happy together, getting lost in each other's eyes whenever they look at each other, I've started to feel that I've been missing something. Yes, I've been with a lot of women, but most of them have given me nothing more than a bit of excitement, great sex. That used to be enough, but not anymore. Now, I've started to wonder how it would feel to have someone to come home to, someone to laugh with, to climb rocks and cliffs with, to work out at the gym with. Someone to share my life with.

The image of Violet pops into my head. I can just imagine waking up next to her in bed, seeing her curls splayed out on the pillow and playing with a few until she wakes up and gazes at me with her sapphire eyes. I can see us working together in the living room, checking each other's numbers. Maybe sometimes we'll argue because she doesn't like being wrong but then I'll shut her up by kissing her and we'll end up having sex on the couch or on the carpet. The scene makes me smile.

But I push it aside. Violet can't even stand to be in the same room as me. How can she be in my life?

I let out a sigh as I bring my glass to my lips. I guess I am jealous.

"I know I am," Ryker confesses.

I give him a puzzled look because I wasn't expecting that. "You are?"

"Don't get me wrong. I don't have a thing for Stella like you did."

My eyebrows arch. "Like I did?"

"You were flirting with her in Switzerland, remember?"

"Only because I wanted to see Ethan's reaction, to gauge his feelings for her and make him do the same."

And I succeeded.

"What I'm jealous of is what they have," Ryker says.

"The baby?"

"The understanding. The bond. I hope I can find someone with whom I can have something like that, someone who can just open up my heart, read my mind and understand my soul."

The longing in his voice takes me by surprise even more. Then again, I shouldn't be surprised. If there's a romantic among the three of us Hawthorne brothers, it's Ryker.

I pat his shoulder. "You will, buddy. I'm sure you will."

Just then, his phone beeps. In the past, I would have scolded him for not putting it on silent mode since we have a rule about that. But hey, Ethan already broke the most important rule.

"Go ahead," I encourage Ryker. "It might be important."

He takes his phone out of his pocket.

"Work?" I ask.

"Actually, no," he answers as he starts to type. "It's Joel."

Unsurprisingly, the name doesn't ring a bell. "Joel? Is that a woman? Someone you're interested in?"

Ryker gives me an annoyed look. "What is it with you and names? Early-onset Alzheimer's? Alcoholic dementia? Joel Parker. My best friend. We went to school together. He used to stay at the house a lot."

"Oh, him."

Now that Ryker has reminded me, I remember the guy perfectly. He was always hanging around Ryker until he left for college. Ethan had no friends. I had a lot of friends. And Ryker had that one friend. Joel, apparently.

I take another sip of my drink. "Doesn't he have a sister? I remember he brought her to a party one time."

Ryker sighs. "Why am I not surprised that that's what you remember about him?"

"She was pretty, wasn't she?"

Ryker answers me with a glare.

I chuckle.

"What's funny?"

"You," I answer. "Looking the same as you did back then when you told me to stay away from her."

"Because she's my best friend's sister," Ryker tells me. "Of course I didn't want you near her."

"Oh, is that why?"

I thought they were dating. I could have sworn they were.

"I didn't want Joel to punch you. And believe me, if you had gone on with your flirting, he would have."

"And you would have let him," I say. "You would have let your best friend punch your own brother."

"Because you deserved it."

"Wow."

"I stopped Ethan from hitting you, didn't I?"

I touch my nose as I remember that incident.

"Maybe next time I won't."

"There isn't going to be a next time," I tell him. "He's in love now, remember? He's happy."

Ryker's phone beeps again. He takes a sip from his drink before reading the message and typing a reply.

"So how's Joel?" I ask. "Didn't you say he became an engineer?"

"Yes. He works for a tech company in California."

"Maybe you should ask him to come work for us now that we're venturing into the tech market, too," I suggest.

He shrugs. "Nah. I think he's perfectly happy where he is."

"But you'll get to see each other more often if you work for the same company."

"Actually, I think we'll be seeing each other more often anyway since the woman he's marrying is from Chicago."

"He's getting married?"

"Next year," Ryker says. "Another man finding his perfect match."

I snort. "If you keep getting all sappy on me, I swear I'm going to leave you here."

He puts away his phone. "Anyway, the wedding will be right here in Chicago, and I'll be the best man."

"And his sister will be there?"

"Of course. You're not getting anywhere near her, though. In fact, you're not invited."

"Don't worry. I wasn't planning on it."

"Because you're still busy trying to convince Violet Cleary to sleep with you?" Ryker asks.

"Sadly, I don't know if that's ever going to happen, but that's fine." I let out a breath. "But that's fine."

Ryker gives me a puzzled look. "It is?"

I finish my drink. "After all, she's leaving the company soon."

Ryker's eyebrows furrow even more. "What? Why?"

"Because she's having a hard time adjusting to her new job," I answer.

Ryker says nothing, but I can feel the suspicion in his piercing gaze.

I shrug. "What?"

"What did you do to her, Asher?"

"What did I do? I didn't do anything. I just told you she's having a hard time ad—"

"The Violet Cleary I know, the Violet Cleary I met in Zurich, doesn't strike me as a woman who has a hard time adjusting to anything. She's damn good at her job. So if she's thinking of quitting, I'm sure it has something to do with you."

"Wow." My eyebrows arch. "Your faith in me is astounding, little brother."

"So what did you do?"

"Nothing," I insist.

If she can't stand me then she has to leave. It's as simple as that.

Ryker sighs. "Well, maybe you have to do something so she doesn't leave. You know Ethan will be pissed if she does. She's really talented. It would be a pity if another company took that talent away from us."

I have to say Ryker has a point.

"What do you want me to do?" I ask him.

"I don't know. You're the one who's good with women."

"Not with this woman." Unfortunately.

He shrugs. "Maybe just be… nice?"

Nice? Like what? Give her flowers? Bring her coffee? Tell her she looks more beautiful now that she's not hiding her blue eyes behind disgusting contacts? Why should I? Even if I do, she'll never forgive me. She'll never be nice to me. What's the point?

"You could give her a welcome present," Ryker suggests.

No way. If I'm going to get her something, it will be the opposite. Something that will piss her off and convince her to quit.

I grin. Well, there's an idea.

~

I'm still trying to think of that perfect present when I reach the floor of my apartment, but my thoughts stop in their tracks as I catch a whiff of something sweet. I turn my head as I realize the scent is coming from the door on my left, the only other door in the hallway apart from mine. I realize what the scent is, too.

Pancakes.

The smell of pancake mix, butter, cinnamon and maple syrup throws me back to a sunlit kitchen. I was six and had a hard time getting on a stool, but I managed on my first try that time. My mother was wearing a white apron over a pink dress and she was humming as she made pancakes. That was one of the few times I remember seeing her well, not pale or in pain or in bed looking so fragile. That was the only time she made something for me, too. I don't think I've ever had pancakes since then.

Nor have I heard of anyone making them at two in the morning. And yet, right now, clearly, someone is. Someone living in the apartment next to mine.

My eyebrows furrow as I stare at the closed door, one which I've passed countless times before but which this time holds a mystery I cannot help but be intrigued by.

I have a neighbor?

I thought I heard a noise coming from the other side of my living room wall the other night, but I didn't think much of it. It definitely didn't cross my mind that I might finally have a neighbor, which I now realize I do.

My lips curve into a grin.

I'm pretty sure my new neighbor is a woman. One who makes pancakes and can't sleep. I like her already.

Who knows? She might just help me forget all about Violet Cleary.

CHAPTER FOUR

Violet

"I almost forgot, Ms. Cleary," Dylan tells me after I leave my final report of the day with him so he can hand it to Asher. I'd do it myself but I'm exhausted enough—I haven't been sleeping much lately what with all the pressure at work—and I really don't want to see his face unless I have to. "Mr. Hawthorne wanted you to have this."

He hands me a rectangular box wrapped in gold paper with a red bow and a small white tag. My name is the only thing written on it.

A present? From Asher?

I throw my puzzled look at Dylan. "But it's not my birthday."

And even if it was, there's no way I'd expect—or accept—a gift from Asher.

"He said it's a welcome present," Dylan explains. "A bit late, he said, but he hopes you'll appreciate it just the same."

A welcome present? After all he's been doing to make me feel unwelcome? After that declaration of war he just issued last week? It can't be.

"You said it's from Mr. Hawthorne?" I ask.

"Yes."

"Mr. Asher Hawthorne?"

Because it could very well be one of the other Hawthorne brothers running this company. That would make more sense. They both seem nicer than Asher. And more reasonable.

"Yes," Dylan answers. "He even bought it himself."

I can understand the surprise I hear in Dylan's tone. Usually, when you're busy enough to warrant an assistant, you let him do your shopping. I'm sure Dylan buys lots of stuff for Asher. That makes this even more suspicious.

Asher is giving me a welcome present? And one that he bought himself, at that? Why? What is he up to?

I can only think of two things. One, this is some kind of prank. True, Asher is a bit too old for pranks—What is he? Thirty at least?—but he acts like a six-year-old, so yeah, I wouldn't put pranks past him.

I press down the edges of the box and give it a shake. It doesn't make much of a sound. Whatever's inside is hard. Compact. That rules out a shirt with weird prints, handfuls of glitter or plastic bugs. Or even live bugs. What is this? One of those glass paperweights with something that looks like animal poop inside? A tumbler with creepy faces? Some cursed antique?

The second possibility is that this is a genuine welcome present. An invitation to start over as coworkers. An olive branch. Maybe Asher has finally come to his senses or maybe he's just grown tired of all our arguments. I know I have, which is why I wouldn't mind a truce. It's about time we set our personal feelings and opinions aside and work side by side for the good of the department and the company.

I really hope that's what it is.

"Thanks," I tell Dylan before bringing the box to my office.

Once I'm behind my desk, I turn my chair around so that I'm facing the wall before starting to unwrap

Asher's present. Most of the people on the floor have gone home, but I still want to make sure no one pries or gets the wrong idea about what I'm doing. There are enough nasty rumors about me going around already, thanks to Asher. I should at least ask him to do something about that if he's serious about wanting to work together.

Finally, all of the wrapping comes off. My pulse races as I stare at the box for a moment.

What can it be?

I draw a deep breath before opening the box. I see what's inside—a rod as pink as a flamingo's feathers, about nine inches long and over an inch in diameter, with a small protrusion on the front shaped like a bunny. I recognize what it is a few seconds later, so I quickly close the box and glance over both my shoulders to make sure no one saw what I just did. There's no one there. Still, my cheeks feel like they're on fire, like they're about to launch off my face. My temper starts to rise as well.

That Asher! That fucking jerk!

I should have known he'd never extend a truce. I should have known that an unreasonable man can't come to his senses, that he can't have a change of heart when he doesn't have a heart in the first place. Damn it. Why did I dare hope? Each time I even consider the notion that he might be human, Asher just tramples all over me and rips me apart. And he's fucking done it again.

Well, I won't let him get away with it this time.

Huffing and puffing, I stomp to Asher's office. Dylan is already gone, his desk cleared. Good. I can yell at Asher all I want, and I fully intend to.

I push the door to his office open and find him behind his desk. His gaze shifts from the screen of his laptop to me. Before he can say anything, I hurl his 'present' at his head as I unleash the words inside mine.

"Du hast den Arsch offen!"

Asher catches the box with one hand and looks at it.

"Oh, I see you got my present." Then he meets my gaze with furrowed eyebrows. "But it seems you don't like it. What's wrong? Is it the color? Is it the size? Would you have wanted it longer? Thicker? Or maybe—"

"What the hell, Asher?" I express my dismay in English as I approach his desk. "What the fuck is this?"

"Oh, you don't know what this is?" He opens the box. "I guess they don't have these in Switzerland."

To my shame, he holds the device up.

"This is a vibrator. A rabbit vibrator, specifically. It's a sex toy that—"

I grab it out of his hand. "For fuck's sake, will you shut up? I know what this is."

"But you asked—"

"I'm asking what you're playing at. Is this another attempt to get me to resign? Quite childish, don't you think? Not to mention desperate."

"It's just a present," Asher says calmly. "It was Ryker's idea, actually."

My eyebrows go up. "What?"

"The gesture, not the toy. That's all me. I even picked it myself."

My hands clench into fists. Here I am feeling horribly insulted, utterly humiliated, my temper bursting at the seams, and he thinks all this is a joke, one he's thoroughly enjoying and feeling extremely proud of. Am I a joke to him? Are decency and honor a joke to him?

"You think all this is amusing, don't you?" I hold up the vibrator. "You think this is funny?"

"No." He clasps his hands on top of his desk. "I think it's well made. It's a work of art, really."

I grit my teeth. "You..."

Just then, I hear a knock on the door. I turn my head. Before Asher can say anything, the door opens and Dylan comes in.

"I'm sorry. I just forgot to..."

He stops as he stares at my hand—my right hand, which still happens to be clutching Asher's gift.

Shit.

I quickly tuck it behind me. But I know I'm too late. Dylan has already seen what I'm holding, and I can tell he knows what he saw. His eyes are wide with disbelief. His cheeks have a tinge of pink.

My head droops from the weight of my embarrassment. I stare at the tips of my red shoes as my toes wiggle inside them, wishing I could just click my heels together and get whisked away to a different place right now.

"Is everything alright?" Dylan asks.

"Oh, we're fine," Asher answers. "Ms. Cleary and I were just having a little argument about the size of our quarterly profits. She thinks they're a bit lacking."

I narrow my eyes at him. What on earth is he talking about?

"Anyway, what did you want?" he asks Dylan in a more serious tone.

Dylan clears his throat. "I just forgot to ask if there was anything else you needed before I left...?"

"There's nothing. You can go."

"Okay."

Dylan leaves. As soon as the door closes, I grab the box on top of Asher's desk and stuff the vibrator back inside.

"I am so reporting you to Human Resources," I tell Asher.

And I mean it this time.

He leans back in his chair. "For what?"

I lift the box in my hand. "Sexual harassment. I'm sure that Gina will help me out. After all, you did say she's a sweet old lady."

"I never said she was old."

I ignore that. "I can just imagine the look on her face when she sees this."

Asher grins. "So can I."

"Think she'll be shocked to find out one of her bosses is a pervert? Then again, she probably already knows. Maybe she's been waiting for someone brave enough to come forward and file a report."

The grin remains on Asher's face as he taps his fingers on his desk. What? Does he think I won't do it? That just makes me even more determined.

I tuck the box under my arm and hold my shoulders back.

"Sending a welcome present isn't sexual harassment," Asher tells me.

"It is when the present is… a sex toy."

Asher shrugs. "Is it wrong for a boss to want his employees to… loosen up a little?"

"Very funny."

"See." He points a finger at me. "That's your problem, Ms. Cleary. You're too serious."

I point a finger at myself. "I'm too serious? Aren't you the one whose forehead looks like it's about to burst whenever I'm around?"

He touches his forehead. I let out a sigh.

"Whatever."

I turn towards the door.

"I'm trying to be nice now," Asher says. "That's why I gave you a present."

I turn back towards him and lift the box. "Oh, so this is your way of being nice?"

"I could have given you a jar of spiders. Or a dead rat."

I shake my head in disbelief. "You're sick."

"Instead, I gave you something you can use, something to help you relax so you can do better at work. Did you know that there are studies saying regular sex can increase one's productivity in the workplace among other benefits?"

I don't care.

"Of course, not all of us can have the luxury of regular sex. Hence the sex toy. And like I said, I've given you one of excellent quality. Raves all around. Completely safe. Easy to use. Easy to clean."

Disgusting.

Asher touches his chin. "Though looking back now, maybe I should have asked for it in purple. Your name's Violet, after all."

Enough of this nonsense.

"Forget this. I'm going and there's nothing you can say or do to stop me."

I start walking towards the door.

"Fine. I'll go with you."

I hear Asher get out of his chair. By the time I glance over my shoulder, he's already almost behind me.

"I can go by myself."

"I'm filing a report, too," he says. "Against you, actually. Physical abuse."

My eyebrows go up. "What?"

"I believe you threw that box at me when you first stormed into my office." He points at it.

I gape. "You caught it."

"So you admit you threw it at me?" He takes his phone out of his pocket. "I've been recording our conversation, by the way."

"Good. Then HR will know just what a jerk you've been."

"Are you sure I've done anything bad or said anything mean to you since you barged into my office? Weren't you the one cursing? What was that you said to me? That I'm full of shit?"

Fuck. I should have known he can understand German.

"That's because you provoked me."

"So you admit you lost your temper and lashed out at your boss?"

"Only because you gave me this... this horrid thing."

I suddenly feel like dropping it on the floor and smashing it to pieces.

"It's called a present, Ms. Cleary."

I narrow my eyes at him. "You know that's not what it is."

"I'm telling you that's what it is." He stands in front of me and looks straight into my eyes. "Or do you want it to be something else, Ms. Cleary?"

The drop in Asher's voice, though just an octave, sends a shiver down my spine. The hint of desire in his ebony eyes makes my breath catch. And I can't seem to take another as I become suddenly aware that his body is just inches from mine.

Too close. I step away and steel my composure.

"I have no idea what you're talking about, Mr. Hawthorne."

"I think you do, Ms. Cleary." His eyes continue to bore down on me. "I think you're insisting on seeing my harmless present as a threat, as a sign that I want to do things to you, an offer to have sex, maybe because that's what you want it to be."

"What?"

Asher leans forward and whispers in my ear. "Do you want to have sex with me, Violet?"

My heart stops. He follows up that question with a gaze pained with longing, and a lump forms in my throat. I swallow.

"Why would I want to have sex with you?"

"Because you didn't get to five years ago."

I snort. "I pushed you away, remember?"

"And yet, you were hurt when I left."

"I was hurt because you just vanished without saying anything. Because you kept me waiting. Because you left me behind. Because I felt like a fool coming to a party in my date's fancy car and going home in an Uber."

"I thought you said I wasn't your date."

I roll my eyes. That's what he picked up from everything I just said?

"So you were waiting for me to come back and pick up where we left off?"

"No."

"Or did you want me to bring you home and then have sex in your room where no one else could see us?"

"No."

"Oh, come on. You wanted to have sex with me that night. You only pushed me away because you were scared."

I open my mouth to answer but no words come out. My mind takes me back to the gazebo on that chilly night.

"You wanted to have sex with me then and you still want to have sex with me now, don't you, Violet?"

The sound of my name from his lips sends another shiver down my spine. The intensity of his gaze lights a fire in my chest that sends heat through my veins so that it spreads throughout my body. The front of my panties starts to burn. My palms tingle. I can't breathe.

Why? Why does Asher still have this effect on me?

He places a finger between his throat and the knot of his tie. He gives it a tug and it loosens.

"Tell me what you want, Violet."

I can't take my eyes off his tie. I suddenly have the urge to grab it and pull Asher close to me so that our lips can collide. I want to take it off along with every piece of clothing he's wearing so I can marvel at his naked body, so I can feel it against mine, on top of mine, just like I've imagined several times before.

Yes. As much as I hate to admit it, I have imagined having sex with Asher before, especially on those cold nights in Zurich when all I had were a bottle of wine and a platter of cheese to keep me company. In spite of all the hurt, I keep going back to that night of Finley's party, to that gazebo, wondering what might have happened if Asher and I did have sex.

I did want it. I still do. But I'm not about to tell him that, especially after everything that's happened these past few days.

That night at that gazebo, I put my thoughts over my feelings. I can do it again.

"I didn't want to have sex with you back then, Asher Hawthorne," I tell him. "That's why I pushed you away. And it's the best decision I've ever made in my life."

"The best decision or the biggest regret?" He crosses his arms over his chest. "Isn't that why you got rid of your contacts? Because you want me to think of you the way I did that night? Because you want to redo it?"

"What?"

Is that what he thinks?

"I started wearing contacts after that night because I didn't want anybody else taking a fancy to me just because I have a rare eye and hair color combination. I didn't want to deal with any other jerks. And the reason why I'm not doing that anymore? Because you're a jerk I've already dealt with. Also, because I want you to remember what you did to me."

"So that I can regret it? I already do."

Does he?

"You have a funny way of showing it."

For a moment, he just looks at me. The lust in his eyes is gone now. But I still see the pain. Is that remorse?

Asher draws a deep breath. "Fine. I won't criticize you in front of others from now on, and I won't steal your ideas."

"And?"

"I'll hear you out whenever you have something to say."

Good. "And you won't ask me to get your coffee, make copies for you, or do any of the other things that Dylan is supposed to be doing?"

"Fine."

I grin. I came to this fight feeling already beaten and about to throw in the towel, and now here I am, winning. It's a good feeling.

I shove the box I'm still holding into Asher's chest. "Then we have nothing more to talk about, Mr. Hawthorne."

I proceed to the door and leave his office with my head held high and the corners of my mouth turned up.

Yup. I'm the one grinning now.

~

I'm still grinning when I get to The Mistral. For the first time in a long time, I feel like I can breathe easily as I walk across the lobby. I don't have to worry about getting bullied at work anymore. Asher might even finally leave me alone. I can do my job in peace and enjoy being in a new city. I may never even have to make pancakes at 2 A.M. because I'll be able to sleep well at night.

I'm free. Well, not of Asher, because he's still my boss. And let's face it. He's a Hawthorne. I may never be able to get his job. But at least I'm free from the past I shared with him. As long as he doesn't hold it against me, I won't hold it against him. It's a fresh start.

We can go on as boss and employee, never interfering with each other's personal lives. Then who knows? Eventually, I may be able to forget about him completely.

I stop in front of the elevator.

Maybe I don't hate Asher. I'm not going to keep punishing him for what he did that night five years ago. But I've learned my lesson. I'm not going to let myself fall for Asher Hawthorne again. He may be hot and smart and maybe he's not completely heartless, but he's still all wrong for me, which is why I'm going to stay away from him from now on. I'm going to have my guard up at all times and keep things strictly professional between us in the office, and as soon as I'm out of that building, I'm going to stop thinking about him. No more fantasies.

The elevator doors open and I step through them. Only the operator, Mitch, is inside.

"Good evening, Ms. Cleary," he says as he presses the button for the thirty-fourth floor.

"I think it will be one," I reply.

I'm going to take a shower, listen to some music while cooking dinner, watch a bit of TV while eating, and then go to bed without a care in the...

"Hold it, Mitch!"

A hand slips between the doors just before they close. Mitch presses the button and they open, giving me a clear view of the man standing outside. My jaw drops.

Asher?

"Violet?" He gives me a puzzled look as he steps inside. "What are you doing here?"

I could ask him the same thing.

"I... live here."

"Oh. Really? So do I."

What? I didn't know that. Stella didn't tell me about it. Besides, I've never seen him here before, though I guess it's entirely possible for two busy people not to bump into each other even if they're living in the same building.

Still, I don't like the fact that we're living in the same building one bit. But I do love my apartment, so as long as he stays out of my way, then...

"You didn't ask Mitch to press the button for your floor," Asher points out.

I look at the button for the thirty-fourth floor. It's still lit.

"Oh, but I did. I..."

I stop as I realize none of the other buttons are lit, which can only mean one thing. No way.

Mitch chuckles. "Congratulations. It looks like you've finally met your neighbor."

What the hell?

CHAPTER FIVE

Asher

"I want her out of The Mistral by tomorrow," I tell Ethan as soon as I find him in his office at the mansion.

He puts down the piece of paper he's holding and lets out a sigh.

"Who did you sleep with this time?"

I frown. "What?"

"The last time you asked for someone to be kicked out of The Mistral, it was a woman you slept with," Ethan reminds me.

I remember. "A woman who turned creepy and started stalking me."

After our one-night stand—and I did make it clear to her that that was all it was—she made it a habit to camp outside my apartment. She would even ambush me whenever I was in the pool or the gym. Worst of all, once while my apartment was being cleaned, she snuck inside and hid in my bathroom, popping up just when I was about to take a shower. I sued her for trespassing and had Ethan kick her out of the building.

"You do have that effect on some women, don't you?" he says. "So, who did you turn into a creep this time?"

"Nobody," I answer. "I haven't slept with anyone staying at The Mistral since then."

"Wow." Ethan's eyebrows arch. "Maybe I should give you a cookie."

I ignore his remark and draw a deep breath.

"I'm talking about Violet Cleary."

Ethan's expression turns serious. "Did you sleep with Violet Cleary?"

Did he not hear what I just said?

"No, but judging from your question, I'm guessing you know she lives at The Mistral."

"I do."

"And do you know she's my neighbor?"

He pauses a moment. "I do."

I give him a puzzled look as I cross my arms over my chest. "Didn't you warn me to stay away from Violet Cleary? And yet you're okay with us being neighbors? What is this? Some kind of test?"

Ethan goes through the papers on his desk. "It's nothing personal, Asher. Violet Cleary is the top executive we gained from the Odermatt acquisition. She needed a place to stay. I felt it was our responsibility to find her one, and the apartment next to yours just happened to be the best option."

"Bull."

Ethan narrows his eyes at me. "I thought you'd be thrilled. Why aren't you? Is it because of your new rule about not sleeping with women who live at The Mistral?"

"You don't have to worry about that. Violet may be attracted to me, but she's determined not to have sex with me, not after she nearly did at a party years ago and I went home with another woman."

Ethan's eyebrows furrow. "Wait. You had met before Zurich?"

"Yes. At Wharton."

"And you were dating?"

"We only went out once and like I said, that ended disastrously."

"And you never thought to tell me?"

"I didn't think it was any of your business," I answer.

"The women you sleep with aren't my business either, but you tell me about them anyway," he points out. "Or is it because you didn't sleep with her? That's why you didn't tell me?"

"I never thought I'd see Violet again," I tell him. "I didn't even recognize her when I met her in Zurich."

"You didn't?"

"She had contacts on. And you know how I am about names."

"I see."

"Anyway, she hates me. She'd sooner hurl herself over a cliff than sleep with me."

"I can see why."

"Then you can see why I can't live with her."

"You're not living with her, Asher," Ethan says. "She's your neighbor."

"Exactly. We live in the same building. On the same floor. I can't have that."

"Because?"

I raise my shoulders. "I already told you. She hates me."

"Lots of neighbors hate each other."

I let out a breath of exasperation. "Ethan."

He taps his fingers on his desk. "You know what? I don't understand. You say she hates you, but you're the one who's here asking for me to kick her out of the building."

"Would you want to live next to someone who hates you?" I ask him. "Anyway, just find her a new place."

I turn towards the door.

"It hurts, doesn't it?" Ethan speaks. "Seeing someone you want every day, knowing you can't have her."

I glance over my shoulder. "Yeah. I know that's how you used to feel. But I had nothing to do with that. Besides, you're not suffering anymore, okay? So just spare me the pain."

"I can't."

What?

"You already dumped her on me at work. I already have to suffer at work. Can't you let me have some peace after work?"

Ethan shrugs. "You can find your own place if you really want."

And leave all my stuff behind? Give up that amazing pool on the rooftop? And the gym that I helped design?

"No."

"Then stop whining like a child and just grow up and deal with it, Asher."

My jaw drops. Didn't he hear a word of what I just said? I came all the way here just to ask for his help. I poured my heart out to him. And this is how he treats me? I'm his brother, for fuck's sake.

"I'm busy." Ethan turns back to his papers. "Are you staying for dinner?"

My jaw clenches. "Fuck you."

I leave his office and slam the door behind me.

I should have known Ethan wouldn't help me. Ever since he got himself a pregnant girlfriend, he's stopped caring about me and Ryker. Well, he can shut himself in his office and rot behind his desk for all I care.

I scratch the back of my head as I walk down the hall. When I see Stella, I stop.

Has she been out here the whole time? Did she hear my conversation with Ethan? It doesn't matter.

I keep walking, but Stella follows me.

"I'm sorry, Asher. I didn't know about your past with Violet when I put her in the apartment next to yours."

So she was listening. Wait. She said she put Violet in the apartment next to mine?

I look at her. "Why did you?"

Stella shrugs. "Because you looked like you really wanted to be with her and I thought maybe if she had the chance to get to know you, she'd like you, too."

"Well, now that you know she already knows me, maybe you can put her somewhere else?"

"Does she? Really know you, I mean. You said you only went out with her once."

"Well, that was enough for her to hate me."

"She hates you for what you did, but maybe if you do other things, if you give her a reason to like you…"

"Look, Stella." I put my hands up. "I know you're just trying to be nice here, but I'm telling you it's not going to work between Violet and me."

Her eyes narrow. "So you're giving up?"

I don't answer. I guess that's what I'm doing, but I don't feel like saying it out loud.

Stella draws a breath. "I know I'm prying, but hey, you didn't exactly leave Ethan and me alone when we were starting out, did you?"

True.

She touches my arm. "You're like a brother to me, Asher. I want you to be happy. And I've spoken to Violet. I really like her. And I think she's lonely, too. I think the two of you would be good for each other."

She does?

"Actually, you're perfect for each other. You're both good with numbers. You're both out to prove something. You both have your walls up."

"Which is exactly why I'm never going to get through to her."

"But have you really tried?" Stella asks me.

Again, I don't answer. She takes my hand and squeezes it.

"I just don't want you to give up before really trying, Asher. If not for Violet then for yourself. I know you regret letting her slip through your fingers in the past. So don't do it again. Try harder. Do better. I know you can."

And I can see the faith in her amber eyes. It makes me want to move mountains. Or at least want to lift a finger in an attempt.

I let out a breath and squeeze her hand back. "Fine. I'll try."

Stella rewards me with a radiant smile. "Good luck."

~

Here goes nothing.

I draw a deep breath before ringing the doorbell. After a few seconds, the door opens. Violet stands in the doorway in a white sweater with the Monte Carlo Casino on it. It's two sizes too big for her, falling off one of her shoulders to reveal the strap of a blue tank top. It reaches almost all the way to her knees, too, making me wonder if she's wearing shorts underneath. Is she?

She isn't wearing any makeup, that's for sure. And yet she looks just as attractive, if not more so. Younger, too. Her blue eyes look more vibrant, her cheeks fuller. Her mass of curls is held back by a cotton headband but a few short strands still dangle over her forehead.

Somehow, I'm reminded of the first time I spoke to her in the library.

"Can I help you?" Violet asks as she pulls her sweater up over her shoulder.

Not the greeting I was hoping to hear. Even 'Hi' would have been preferable. 'Can I help you?' is usually reserved for people who knock on your door to ask for directions or sell something, people you weren't expecting, people you'd rather not waste time on. But I guess it will have to do.

"Hey." I give her a smile. "I didn't see you leave the office earlier. What time did you go home?"

"Um…" Violet purses her lips as she fidgets with the neckline of her sweater. "Six?"

I nod. "Anyway, I just wanted to give you this."

I offer her the box in my hands, which I didn't have wrapped this time so she can clearly see what it is. She looks at it with creased eyebrows and reads the words on the cardboard.

"Pancake molds?"

"Yeah. They're a welcome present. Or a moving-in present. Or a housewarming present. Whatever you call it. You know, the thing your new neighbor gives you after you've just moved into your new home."

Violet just keeps staring at the box.

I extend my hand. "I promise the contents are…"

"I can't." She shakes her head as she takes a step back. "I appreciate the gesture and all, but I can't accept this gift."

I thought she'd say that. Still, I'm not backing down easily, not after Stella told me to really try to get through to Violet.

"Why not?"

"Because…"

She clutches the front of her sweater as she searches for her words. The neckline dips and my gaze goes to the hollow of her throat. Pale. Smooth. Pristine. Exactly the kind of place I'd love to press my lips against.

"Well, because I don't make pancakes," Violet says.

Liar. "Really? Because I'm pretty sure that's what I smelled when I passed by your apartment last weekend."

Her eyebrows arch. "What time?"

"Around 2 A.M."

She looks away and purses her lips. Yup, that's the look of someone who's been caught lying. But I'll let her off the hook this time.

"They smelled good, by the way," I simply add.

She touches the nape of her neck as she meets my gaze for a second, a tentative smile on her lips.

"Th–Thanks."

"Maybe next time you make them, you can use the molds. Or not. It's your choice. Either way, I'm sure you make great ones, so if you have a hard time finishing them, you can invite me over and—"

"No." Violet shakes her head.

"Okay. You can finish them all and—"

"We can't do this," she cuts me off. "It's not right. You're my boss."

"I'm your neighbor, too."

"Well, you don't have to be. I mean, you don't have to act like one." She fidgets with the front of her sweater. "We already have to... endure each other's company at work. We don't have to do that when we're here. We can just pretend we're strangers. We don't have to check up on each other. We don't have to cook for each other or exchange recipes or ask for ingredients or feed each other's pets or invite each other for drinks or stop by for chats or any of that stuff that neighbors do."

I stay silent. I've only been half listening, the other half of my attention drawn to Violet's slender fingers. I never noticed she had such graceful hands or that she has a tiny tattoo on her wrist—an inverted capital letter E followed by three dots forming an invisible triangle and then the infinity symbol. A trio of mathematical symbols. Interesting.

I've been with women with tattoos, some of whom liked to show theirs off and brag about how profound they were, but this is the first time I've seen this kind of tattoo. What's even more interesting is that I, too, have a mathematical symbol tattooed on my back.

Stella's right. Violet and I are perfect for each other.

"Say something," she urges me.

I meet her gaze. "Do you know that you talk too much when you're anxious?"

Her blue eyes grow wide. I'm guessing she doesn't.

"I do not," Violet protests.

"Yes, you do. You remember at Finley's party when you were talking to Ron Lenning, one of the President's former financial advisors? You couldn't stop talking about his economic policies and programs. And when we met the author of your favorite book—What was his name again?"

"Godwyn Klein."

"You practically quoted a whole paragraph he wrote."

Violet frowns. "I did not."

"Yes, you did."

She sighs. "Fine. I talk a lot when I'm anxious. Happy now?"

I chuckle. "Don't worry. You still look hot even when you talk a lot."

Her eyes narrow. "Are you making fun of me?"

"And when you're angry."

She puts her hands on her hips. "You are making fun of me."

I'm not. I mean it. I don't think I've ever found her not hot, not even when she was talking trash about me at the café or when she gave me the cold shoulder in Zurich or when she was mean to me the day she arrived in Chicago. It doesn't matter whether she's oozing with confidence or a little frazzled, busy at a computer or staring into space, in a suit, in a dress or in a T-shirt and shorts. There's just something about her that I can't seem to resist.

Even now, it's taking all of my strength not to pull her into my arms and kiss her, claim her lips and drink her every breath until she's reeling and stumbling back so I can whisk her off her feet and carry her to the bed.

Fuck.

"What are you looking at?" Violet asks.

"You," I admit.

She blushes. Ah. She looks hot when she does that, too.

Besides, blushing is a sign that I'm winning her over. Just a little more.

I take a step forward. "You know when I first found you attractive?"

Violet doesn't answer, so I proceed.

"Management Communication. That first meeting when Dr. Simmons asked us all to give a little speech about something we cared about. You were wearing a white blouse with a lace collar and pleats, puffy sleeves, black pants. You spoke about gender equality, how men still dominate the corporate workplace, how women can do just as well. Your passion was just... searing."

Her eyes widen slightly. I hold her gaze as I lift my hand to touch her cheek.

"You know what I wanted to do then? This."

I lean forward and press my lips to Violet's. No reaction. I kiss her more firmly as I stroke her cheek. Ever so slightly, she kisses me back. A thrill rushes down my spine. The box in my hand drops to the floor.

I cradle her jaws with both hands as I crush her mouth. She clutches the front of my shirt. Over and over, our lips collide, and when she parts hers, I push my tongue in. It brushes against the tip of her tongue and heat sizzles in my veins.

Damn, I want her.

Suddenly, the hands on my chest try to push me back. She tries to pull her face away as well.

Not again.

This time, I ignore her resistance and cup her face firmly as I pin her tongue down. I know she wants this. She wants me, too. I've seen it in her eyes. I just have to make her swallow her pride long enough to admit it.

She doesn't. She just pushes even harder, and when I finally step back, she rewards me with a slap on my cheek and a knee to my groin.

What the fuck?

As the door slams in my face, I fall to the floor writhing in pain. I clutch my balls first, then my stomach, which feels like it's turning inside out, burning and getting ripped to pieces all at the same time. My vision blurs. My head spins.

As my thoughts get muddled, most slipping away, one remains clear.

I'm going to make sure Violet pays for this.

CHAPTER SIX

Violet

Maybe I shouldn't have done that to Asher.

Remorse pricks me like a dozen needles as I crouch under the covers of my bed, which is where I've been hiding since I kicked Asher out of my apartment.

Kicked out? No. That's not the right word. Slapped. Shoved. With my knee. To his groin.

Just the thought of how that must have felt for him makes me grimace as I lie on my back.

I am such a horrible, horrible person.

I didn't mean to do it, I swear. I just... panicked when I realized I was doing the one thing I shouldn't be doing. My adrenaline kicked in. Fight or flight. I tried to flee but Asher wouldn't let me so I fought back. I slapped him. And then buried my knee in his groin.

I grip my hair. What have I done?

No matter what my excuse, I shouldn't have done that. I should have just slammed the door in his face after telling him I didn't want to play neighbors instead of falling under his spell again, getting myself carried away to the past before he broke my heart. I didn't send him away soon enough. I lowered my guard, so he attacked. I let him in and then remembered I wasn't supposed to so I tried to throw him over the wall. Which I did. And now, I feel sorry for it.

Not the slapping. He deserved that for not pulling away immediately when I started pushing him back. But the attack on his balls. That was too much.

What if his balls got broken? I mean what if they ruptured? What if he can never ejaculate again?

The more I think about it, the more the guilt gnaws at me. I get an urge to go next door to check on Asher, make sure he's alright, but no. I have a feeling I'm the last person he wants to see right now. What do I do, then? Call 911 just in case he needs a doctor? What if he's bleeding to death right now? Then again, if I call 911, the police might find out what I did. I could go to jail.

Fuck.

On second thought, I might not go to jail if I plead self-defense. But if I do that, won't Asher be in trouble?

I shake my head. No. I'm not going to call 911. And I'm not going to check on him. He's fine. I'm sure he is. Well, maybe not right now. Right now he must be in a world of pain. But he will be fine after he gets some rest and takes some pain relievers. Right?

Right. Asher is a strong, well-built man. He'll be fine. I'm sure he'll show up for work tomorrow. And when he does, I'll apologize profusely. I'll even bow my head and all and offer to do his work for him. He'll have to forgive me, right?

I sigh.

Just to be on the safe side, maybe I'll make pancakes.

~

I grip the container filled with a week's worth of pancakes in my hand and take a deep breath before knocking on the door to Asher's office.

"Come in," he says.

I step inside. I find Asher behind his desk just like last time, in another crisp suit. Good. He looks fine.

He turns his head to look at me but says nothing. I open my mouth.

"I..."

"You should find somewhere else to stay," he blurts out as he turns back to his computer screen.

My eyebrows arch. What?

"You're old enough to find a place of your own, aren't you? Besides, you've been in Chicago for... two weeks already, right? You should know the city by now."

Not really. I've been mostly staying either here at the office or in my apartment. I haven't had time to go sightseeing.

"Don't worry. Wherever it is, it should be cheaper than the Mistral. In the meantime, you can stay at a hotel, which the company will pay for. Sounds good?"

Good? He wants me to move out of the apartment that I've fallen in love with and stay at a hotel until I find somewhere smaller and farther away from here. How can that be good?

"That's..."

"You can take the afternoon off to move your things."

Wow. He really can't wait to get me out of his building, can he? Plus it seems he's reached a new level of being unreasonable.

I know I did something wrong. I'm willing to apologize for it, to make up for it. I promise never to do it again. But it's not like what happened is entirely my fault. And it definitely doesn't warrant a punishment this severe.

I hold my chin high. "I'm not moving out."

Asher looks at me. "I don't believe I gave you a choice."

I draw a breath. "It's not your choice to give. It's mine to make. And I choose not to move out."

His eyebrows arch. "Wow. I knew you were stubborn. Obstinate. I didn't think you were... shameless."

"I'm not," I tell him. "I am very sorry for what I did to you and I promise it will never happen again. If you want me to clean your apartment for a week, cook meals for you, get you coffee or take on extra work, I'd be happy to. But I'm not moving out."

"So you're not really sorry."

"I am," I insist. "But I think kicking me out of the building is too much."

It's unfair, really.

"You mean like shoving your knee into my groin?"

I frown. "Like I said, I'm sorry for what I did."

Asher leans back in his chair and narrows his eyes at me. "Are you, Ms. Cleary?"

"But I'm not the only one who should be sorry. Don't you think so, Mr. Hawthorne?"

His eyebrows furrow as dismay flickers in his ebony eyes. "Are you saying this is my fault?"

"I'm saying part of it is," I answer. "After all, you were the one who came to my apartment."

"You let me kiss you," Asher points out.

True. "And then I tried to push you away."

"You mean like you did last time? You haven't changed. You're still such a cocktease."

"And you still can't handle rejection."

Asher falls silent but his gaze speaks volumes. He hates me. I can feel it. This isn't just him being annoyed at me like he's been before or him trying to be mean. I can see the pain in his eyes. He's hurt. I hurt him—and I don't mean just physically—so now he hates me. And I expected it. I told myself I could handle it, but that cold gaze stabs my chest more than I thought it would. Still, I keep my shoulders square as I look right into his eyes.

"I'm not moving out."

His eyebrows twitch slightly. "I thought you didn't want us to be neighbors. Or is that another thing you say you don't want but deep down inside, you really do?"

Asher leans forward on his desk.

"Have you always been like this? Do you ever mean yes when you say yes and no when you say no? Or is it always maybe yes, partly no?"

I keep quiet. I was already prepared for a lecture when I entered Asher's office. And if enduring his harsh words is my price to pay for him letting me stay at The Mistral, I don't mind it.

"I know I sleep around, but I never lead women on or leave them hanging. That's just pointless and exhausting. And cruel. But you seem to get a kick out of it."

Ouch.

"Or do you? In spite of everything you've done, shoving your knee in my groin included, you don't strike me as a heartless person, which makes me wonder. Are you really a secret sadist, or are you just a child disguised as a grown woman, clueless about what she really wants?"

I draw a breath as I try to shove his words aside.

"I never said I didn't want us to be neighbors. I said we don't have to act like neighbors just because we've realized we are. We can just go back to how we were when we didn't know about it."

"You don't mind living next to someone you hate?"

I already know I don't hate him, but I don't tell him that.

"Or someone who resents you?"

So I'm right. He hates me now. Well, I'll just have to live with that.

"I'm not moving out, Mr. Hawthorne," I tell him again.

Asher shrugs. "Fine."

Fine. I let out a breath as I turn around. That didn't go that badly, did it?

"But Ms. Cleary."

Of course Asher isn't done yet.

I glance over my shoulder. "Yes?"

The gleam in his eyes looks like hell frozen over, making me nearly shudder.

"You're going to wish you did."

~

I am starting to wish I had moved out.

I cover my ears with the sides of my pillow after I hear another bang against the wall. They're still at it? Seriously? Haven't they been at it for... what, three hours now? That's even longer than last time.

And louder, I think as I hear another bang.

I turn over so that I'm lying on my stomach and pull my pillow over my head in hopes that it will muffle the noise. It doesn't.

I roll my eyes. You'd think that with the high rent, the rooms at The Mistral would have thicker walls.

Just then, I hear a scream. Or is that a screech? A howl? Do people even howl? If I wasn't pissed, I would laugh at it, but since I am, I frown. Whatever that sound is, it's weird. And unusually loud.

That's right. It's not the fault of the building that it's noisy in my bedroom right now. Asher and whoever it is he's with are just being extremely loud. And I'm guessing it's on purpose.

The purpose? To drive me out of my mind, of course. And maybe my apartment.

That's exactly why Asher has brought home a woman every night for the past several nights. And I mean every night. Once, I think he even brought two. Who does that? And each time, he makes it a point to let me know. The banging on the walls. The laughter. The moans. The screams. And there goes another one just now.

I wonder if Asher makes it a point to pick women who are loud, like he asks them if they're loud in bed after they tell him their names—hilarious—or if he orders them to scream at the top of their lungs whenever he's... doing whatever he's doing to them. Because seriously, the noise is unreal. Asher can't be that good.

Or is he?

I've tried not to mind the whole thing. The first time, I simply did my best to ignore the noise. And the images. Frankly, I think the images do more damage. I couldn't. No one is that mentally tough. So the next night, I played music. Loud rock ballads. But I've never been a fan of rock and I've never been good at sleeping with music on, or doing anything with music on for that matter. So yeah, I didn't get any sleep then either. The third night, I got earbuds, only to remove them after a few minutes because I couldn't sleep with them on. They just felt weird.

After three nights of barely any sleep, I decided to spend the fourth in the living room. I finally did manage to get some sleep there, but I woke up with back pains which bothered me the whole day. I moved to the spare bedroom the following night only to get bitten by bedbugs. Great.

So here I am back in my bedroom as I should be. If I let Asher drive me out of my bedroom, who's to say he won't succeed in driving me out of my apartment next?

But damn it, I can't stand the noise. And the images.

As the noises grow louder, the images in my head become more vivid. I imagine Asher pounding this loud, faceless woman up against the wall, her legs wrapped around his waist, her arms around his neck. I can see the beads of sweat on his back and the scratch marks from her nails from earlier. I can see the muscles moving, creating ripples in his skin. His pale, perfect, round ass doesn't jiggle one bit as he jerks his hips.

I lick my lips.

The woman screams again. Even louder this time. She must be close. Then I hear another thud on the wall.

Asher must have put her down on the floor and turned her around. He's fucking her from behind now. Hard. The woman's hands are above her head, her wrists pinned by one of Asher's hands. His other hand is on her breast. He squeezes it firmly as he jerks his hips. Heat floods my chest.

Each time Asher moves his hips, heat travels through my veins until it reaches every corner of my body. My breasts swell against the sheets. My belly catches fire.

The sound of skin slapping against skin fills the air. And something wet. I reach between my legs and feel a wet spot on my underwear. I rub against it and shiver.

Asher's jaw clenches. His nostrils flare. Pure lust swims in the dark orbs peeking from beneath heavy eyelids. Then he opens his mouth.

"I'm... coming."

My fingers move faster as Asher's hips pick up speed. They stop and lips part. My body trembles as ripples of pleasure travel beneath my skin.

The woman cries out. Only, as my mind starts to clear, I realize it wasn't the woman.

It was me. I made that sound. I... came. While listening to Asher have sex with another woman on the other side of the wall, imagining it was me.

Fuck.

I sit up and clasp my hand over my mouth as shame washes over me. Then I realize my fingers are wet. I stare at them and my stomach tightens. I suddenly feel sick.

What was I doing?

I run to the bathroom to wash my hands. I don't look at my reflection in the mirror. I can't bear to. I'm disgusted with myself for masturbating to the noise of my neighbors having sex. And not just any neighbors. Asher. I let him win. I let him take control of me without even touching me.

Does he have this much power over me? Or am I just that weak? At any rate, I feel like pounding my head against the bathroom wall.

Instead, I simply rest my forehead against the cold tiles. Once my temper has cooled somewhat and my breathing is no longer jagged, I step out. But then I hear more moaning from the other side of the wall and my temper simmers again.

No fucking way.

I've had enough, so I stomp over to the next apartment. I almost bring a knife, but I'm afraid I might end up committing murder, so I bring a pan instead. I bang that on Asher's door.

After a few seconds, Asher appears. He runs his fingers through the waves of his sweat-drenched hair.

"Hey. What's up?"

Against my will, my eyes dart towards Asher's crotch, which thankfully is covered with part of a blanket. I mentally kick myself as I pull my gaze away—only to have it drawn to his bare chest instead, a ripped chest with a thin layer of hair running straight down the middle.

"Nice pan," he says.

I transfer my gaze to it. "I thought I... heard something."

"And you thought you'd give it a whack with a pan?"

I suddenly feel stupid, so I hide the cooking tool behind me.

Asher grins. "Don't worry. It was just me and Carina having sex. Wild, kinky, mind-blowing sex."

His choice of adjectives lights a fire in my cheeks. Damn him.

"Would you like to join in? I think we have room for one more."

I look at him with narrowed, disgusted eyes. My fingers tighten around the handle of my pan.

"You know what? I should have smashed your balls when I had the chance."

"You should have left the building when you had the chance. Or the company. Or the country."

"I'm not moving out of anything," I tell him firmly.

"Right." He scratches his chin. "Because you can't stay away from me, can you?"

My temper rises even more. "Bullshit."

He leans against the door frame. "Why are you here, then?"

"You know why I'm here."

"Because you got tired of just getting off on the sounds of me having sex and decided you want a piece of the action?"

My eyes grow wide as my cheeks turn red. How did he know I was...? I shake off the rest of the thought and glare at him.

"Because I heard you fucking like animals."

"Why, thank you." Asher mocks me with a grin. "That's what real sex is like. Don't you know? Oh wait. You don't. You've never had sex."

"I have."

"Real sex? The kind that makes your toes curl, that makes every inch of your skin tingle..." His gaze travels down my body. "That makes you tremble beyond control until you lose your mind and can't even remember your own name?"

I don't answer because I have a lump in my throat.

"I'm guessing no," Asher says. "That's why you're jealous, aren't you?"

I swallow. "I am not jealous."

His eyes goad me beneath furrowed eyebrows as his grin widens. "Are you sure?"

I take the pan out from behind me and lift it with both hands. My jaw clenches. My shoulders tremble in anger.

"Wanna hit me with that pan? Go ahead." Asher extends his arms. "You can't hurt me any more than when you buried your knee in my balls."

His offer is tempting. Very tempting. But I put the pan down.

"I'm not a monster like you."

With the pan in hand, I march back to my apartment. I throw it on the couch. Then I sit on the living room rug and bury my face in my hands.

I fucking hate you, Asher Hawthorne.

At least, right now, I really wish I could.

CHAPTER SEVEN

Asher

I stay in the doorway staring out into the hall even after Violet has disappeared into her apartment. I should be proud and happy because the fact that she came to my door to complain about my noisy night adventures means my plan has succeeded. I've made her life difficult, and though she insists she's staying, I can tell she's starting to think about moving out of the building. But I don't feel even a sliver of joy or pride or accomplishment. I just feel like the monster she says I am.

Is that what she really thinks of me? Is that what I really am?

"Hey," Carina calls me.

I glance over my shoulder to see her draped in the white duvet like a Greek goddess. She gives me a devilish grin.

"Are we going to continue or what?"

I stare at her. I've been with her for the past few hours but it feels like I'm looking at her for the first time. She has a nice, full figure, I'll give her that.

And luscious curls. Plus she was good in bed. And on the floor. And against the wall. Yet I don't feel the slightest spark of attraction towards her now.

"You should go," I tell her.

Her thin eyebrows arch. "What?"

"You should go," I repeat as I step aside to give her a better view of the exit.

Carina frowns as she puts a hand on her hip. "You said you could go for a few more rounds."

Did I?

"Maybe I can, but I don't want to anymore," I tell her.

Frankly, I suddenly feel tired.

She puts her other hand on her hip. The duvet falls to the floor.

"Sure?"

"Sure," I answer without any hesitation even as I look at her naked body.

Carina sighs. "Fine."

She starts to pick up her clothes, which are scattered all over the living room.

"My throat's getting a little hoarse anyway, what with you constantly telling me to be louder."

I say nothing. She puts on her underwear and her pants.

"Who was that banging on the door?"

I nearly grin as I remember the sight of Violet with that pan. She could have brought a rolling pin. Or a spatula. Or an umbrella. Instead, she brought a pan. Not that she needs a weapon, as she already proved last week. The memory of what she did with just her knee is still enough to make me wince.

"Just my neighbor," I answer Carina's question. "She thought I was wrestling with a burglar or something."

Carina snorts before putting on her blouse. "Stupid. Didn't she hear me moaning through the wall?"

I frown. It's weird. I've said a lot of mean things to Violet without flinching, yet all Carina did was call her stupid and I feel like I've been hit in the balls once again.

I feel like throwing her out of my apartment, but I wait patiently by the door for her to finish getting fully clothed.

"Anyway, that was fun," she says as she puts on her coat. "I had fun."

No comment.

She slips her feet into her shoes. "So much fun that I wouldn't mind doing it again."

"You know I don't do seconds," I tell her. "I told you before we started."

"Right." She grabs her purse. "I usually don't either, except this time, I—"

"No seconds, Carina," I cut her off.

It doesn't matter how good the sex is. When you sleep with a woman more than once, she starts to get ideas inside her head. The next thing you know, she's threatening to kill you if you leave.

Carina nods slowly. "Fine."

She walks towards the door but stops in front of me.

"It was a real pleasure spending time with you, Asher," she whispers in my ear.

Then she puts her hand on my chest and plants a kiss on my cheek. She's about to press her lips against mine, too, but I grab both her arms and push her away. Yes, I liked her enough to have sex with her, but now that the sex is over, I'm starting to find her annoying, especially since she's obviously stalling her departure.

"Good night," I tell her as I look into her eyes, trying to convey the message that I want her to leave so I don't have to say it.

She smiles in understanding and walks out but stops just outside the door and turns around before I can close it.

"That woman, your neighbor," Carina says. "You're in love with her, aren't you?"

My eyebrows furrow. What?

"I'm not," I assure her.

She grins. "Really?"

Now she's just unbearable.

"Goodbye, Carina."

I close the door before she can come up with any more nonsense. Then I head to the bathroom to take a shower. As the drops of water crash down on my skin, I think of what Carina said.

Me? In love with Violet? How ever did she come up with that idea?

I'm not. I just want to have sex with her. That's all. I just want to know how it would feel to have her bare body trembling against mine, to look into her cobalt blue eyes as I bury myself deep inside her, to hear my name leave her lips in a gasp. I just want her to let go of all her fears and inhibitions and feel good.

Why? Because I don't think she understands what pleasure means. She's too serious. She expects too much of herself. She's too careful, too defensive. For once, I want her to take a chance. Take a leap. Break through her own walls and be reckless, fearless. I know she can. If only she could open her heart, she'd see that as well, but she's blinded by doubts and fears. I know that feeling, too.

Violet may not see it, but we have a lot in common. We're both stubborn to a fault. We've both been hardened by the years. We both hate showing any sign of weakness. I have no doubt we'd both be amazing in bed.

That doesn't mean I intend on having sex with her for more than one night. More than one round, sure. More than one night, no. I'm not going to start a relationship with her. Like I said, I'm just after the sex, and once that's done, I'll leave her alone just like all the women I've slept with for the past several years. I'm never going near her again, not even if she comes to my door like she did earlier and wears that face, that face desperately trying to keep tears at bay as she threatened me with a pan. Fuck, I wanted to pull her into my arms then.

But only because I felt guilty. That's all. I know I can be a jerk sometimes, but no one has impressed that fact upon me more than Violet. Maybe because no one brings that side of me out more than she does. She frustrates me. She makes me lose my temper. She makes me feel like a kid and makes me do stupid things. She drives me out of control. She…

I stop and let out a laugh that bounces off the tiles. What am I thinking? That Violet has control over me?

No. That's absurd. No woman can control Asher Hawthorne.

Starting now, I'm going to act more like myself instead of reacting to Violet. I'm going to stop going out of my way to be mean to her. I'm going to stop trying to hurt her or make her leave. I'm going to stop asking, expecting things from her. I've grown tired of all of it anyway.

Ever since Violet arrived from Switzerland, I've been all about her. Trying to get her to sleep with me. Trying to annoy her. Enough.

No more plots. No more stupid arguments. No more games.

Starting tomorrow, Violet is going to see the real Asher Hawthorne.

~

"Good morning, Ms. Cleary," I greet Violet as I put a cup of coffee on her desk before heading to my office.

She looks up at me with wide eyes. I smile.

"What's this?" she asks as she glances at the cup of coffee.

"Cappuccino," I answer. "With vanilla foam and a bit of cinnamon. I thought you might need it."

Violet says nothing. I can tell from her expression that she's trying to guess my intention. Am I genuinely being nice to her after being an ass last night? Or am I making fun of her?

"Don't worry," I tell her. "I didn't put anything in it."

I'd never do that, but I can understand why she's reluctant to believe me after all the other things I've tried. It's best to give her a few moments to make up her mind.

"Good day, Ms. Cleary." I start to walk away from her desk. "Oh, and kindly give me a copy of the report on our estimated expenses for the next quarter this morning so I can take a look at it before the meeting with Ethan this afternoon. You can just hand it to Dylan and then I'll have it sent back to you if there are any changes necessary."

Again, Violet just gives me a wide-eyed look. I wonder what she's more surprised about—the fact that I'm acting like her boss or that I said 'kindly'.

"Is that alright, Ms. Cleary?" I ask.

"Y–yes, sir," she answers. "I'll have the report ready for you in an hour."

Now that's more like her.

"Good. I'll be expecting it."

I give her one last smile before heading to my office.

Violet

I frown at the ceiling as I lie in bed.

It's weird. I should be sleeping peacefully right now because I haven't been getting a lot of sleep lately and it's finally quiet on the other side of the wall. I should even have a smile on my lips because today was a good day.

Asher got me a nice cup of coffee. He helped me with my report. He backed me up in front of his brother during the meeting and as a result I got praised by the CEO. Then after the meeting, Asher let me go home early, which allowed me to cook a nice dinner, have a longer shower and get to bed early.

In short, Asher was good to me all day. Kind. And all I can do is keep wondering why. What is he up to this time?

There must be a reason. When the girl who's always a bitch to you sits next to you at lunch, it's usually because she wants to copy your homework. When the quarterback who doesn't know you exist suddenly approaches you at your locker and says he likes your hair, it's usually because he's bored with his current girlfriend or trying to make her jealous. When your mother stops making breakfast for you every morning and tucking you into bed every night and starts drinking every day until she just stares into space and doesn't recognize you, it's because your father cheated on her.

There's always a reason. The problem is I don't know what Asher's is. Is he trying to kill me with kindness? Is this a new ploy to get rid of me? Or is he just trying to get me to like him so that I'll sleep with him?

I don't know. I wish I did. Then I'd know what to expect and how I'm supposed to respond. But I can't read another person's mind. It's confusing, frustrating, maddening.

It's impossible.

A yawn escapes my mouth. I turn on my side, hug my pillow and close my eyes.

I should stop torturing myself trying to do it, then. God knows I've been tortured enough these past few days. Besides, it may only be a phase.

Tomorrow, Asher might go back to being the jerk I know.

~

He didn't.

It's the end of the week and Asher is still wearing that halo around his head. He's been bringing me coffee. He's been helping me with work. He's been letting me go home early. And I'm really curious why.

Maybe I should just ask him?

Just then, I hear a knock on the door to my office. I look up and find Asher standing outside the glass.

Speaking of the devil. Or should I say the angel?

I open the door. "Sir?"

"I think you should go through these numbers again."

He hands me the tablet. I look at the screen, which displays a chart from the report I submitted earlier. It takes me only a few seconds to see the error and gasp in dismay.

How could I have made such a glaring mistake?

"I'm so sorry, sir," I apologize at once. "I'll correct it right away."

I wait for the scolding. Instead, I get a look of concern.

"Are you feeling alright, Ms. Cleary?" Asher asks me. "You don't usually make mistakes like this."

"I know. I'm fine. I just... had a mental lapse, I guess. And no, I'm not making excuses. It's a mistake, my mistake, and I will fix it."

Asher smiles. "No worries."

'No worries'? Before this week, it would have been 'You better' or 'It better not happen again'.

Asher's eyebrows furrow. "Is something wrong, Ms. Cleary? You look a little confused."

I am. More than a little.

"Any questions?"

Who are you and what have you done with Asher Hawthorne?

"I was just wondering..." I pause to draw a breath. "If there's something you wanted me to do."

He nods. "Yes. I want you to fix that mistake."

"No. I mean yes, I will do that. But is there... anything else you want from me?"

He scratches his chin. "Let's see. That data analysis I mentioned the other day?"

"I mean something that's not related to work," I clarify as simply as I can.

"Oh." He pauses for a moment to think, then shakes his head. "No. I can't think of anything. Why?"

"Nothing," I answer quickly.

Maybe I shouldn't have asked.

His eyes narrow. "Did I, without my knowledge, make you think I want something from you, Ms. Cleary?"

I suddenly feel stupid. What if I'm reading too much into his behavior? What if he's just being kind? There's no reason required for someone to be kind, right?

"No, sir," I tell him. "Please forget what I said."

"Are you sure?"

I nod.

"Because just to be clear, I'm not expecting anything from you apart from your hard work."

Of course. I'm just imagining otherwise because I can't accept the fact that I suddenly have a nice boss. I'm the one who's not right in the head. Not Asher.

"I understand."

"What about you, Ms. Cleary?" he asks. "Is there something you want from me?"

I pause. Is there?

I shake my head. "No, sir."

"Not even another cup of coffee?" he offers.

"No, thank you." I glance at the cup on my desk, which is still a quarter full. "One is enough."

"Okay."

Asher walks away, then stops and glances over his shoulder.

"By the way, Ms. Cleary…"

I lift my chin. "Yes?"

"Nice dress."

~

Nice dress?

I take a moment to examine how it looks in the mirror of the women's restroom as I wash my hands after lunch.

I guess it does look nice. A white pencil dress with blue orchids, a boat neckline and a gold lace sash. It's Friday, after all. I usually wear my nicest dresses on Fridays.

What doesn't happen usually? Asher paying me a compliment. What's next? Is he going to buy me flowers? Ask me out on a date? And if he does, what do I do? Can I still refuse after how kind he's been to me? Has that been his plan all along—to be so kind to me that I'll feel indebted and do anything for him? I know he said he wasn't expecting anything from me, but I can't help but feel that I'm obliged to do something in return.

I shake my head. Now I'm really confused. I don't know how to deal with this kind Asher. I've never been good at dealing with kind people. That's why I barely have friends or go home to spend time with my family.

I can deal with jerks. I can deal with envious colleagues. I can deal with arrogant superiors and incompetent subordinates. But kind people? Their very existence confuses me.

And now, Asher is one of them. So what on earth do I do about him?

The mirror doesn't give me an answer so I get out of the restroom. As I pull the handle of my purse over my shoulder in the corridor, I nearly bump into a woman on her way in.

"Sorry," I mumble.

The woman, an auburn-haired, pear-shaped thirty-something in a rust-colored top and black skirt, says nothing. She just stops and stares at me.

My eyebrows crease. "Do I know you?"

"No." She continues in a softer but somehow resentful voice as she gets out of my way. "But I know you."

Hmm. At first, I decide to ignore the comment and keep walking, but I change my mind after a few steps. When I stop to look over my shoulder, I find the woman and two of her friends whispering. One of them glances at me.

Oh, they're definitely talking about me. Maligning me, from the looks of it. Now, I've had to put up with a lot of crap since I joined this company, mostly from Asher, but now that he's respecting me like he should, I'm not tolerating any of it any longer.

"Hi." I give the women a wide smile as I walk over to them. "Is there something you'd like to talk to me about? If you have something you're brave enough to say to my face, I'm happy to listen."

Two of the women, including the one I nearly bumped into, fall silent. The third, a brunette in a pink blouse, puts on a smile that rivals mine, too wide to be real.

"We were just... talking about... your lipstick. It looks nice. What brand is it?"

"Oh. It's..."

I start to get the tube from my purse but stop when I notice the auburn-haired woman rolling her eyes. Oh no she didn't.

"Is there something else you'd like to ask?" I ask her because she looks like she's dying to say her piece. "Now's your chance."

She looks at me. "Are you going out with Asher Hawthorne?"

Now, that wasn't so hard.

"No," I answer.

"You don't intend to?" she asks next.

"No. So if you want to have a go at him—"

"Then why do you keep leading him on? Why do you have him at your beck and call?"

What? "That is not true."

"I heard he brings you coffee every morning. Is that not true?"

Is that what this is all about?

"It is, but…"

"And that he lets you go home early so you can relax while he does all of your work?"

I frown. "He does not."

The woman folds her arms beneath her breasts. "He used to hate you. He couldn't stand seeing you, and now all of a sudden he's like… your puppy. And yet you say you're not going out with him and don't intend to. So you're just using him to get ahead? Is that it? Are you sleeping with him in exchange for favors?"

Wow. That's a lot of stuff she's been dying to say. Well, now it's my turn.

I draw a breath. "For the record, I am not—"

"Ms. Cleary is not sleeping with me to get ahead," Asher says as he emerges from around the corner.

My eyebrows arch. How long has he been standing there? How much did he hear?

"In fact, she's not sleeping with me at all," Asher goes on. "Which is perfectly fine with me."

It is? I thought he wanted me to have sex with him? Did he change his mind?

"I've been bringing her coffee to make up for the fact that I was a jerk to her during her first weeks here just like you said. And because I've noticed she hasn't been getting a lot of sleep. And you know why not? Because Ms. Cleary works very hard, even when she's not in the office. I know for a fact that she's busy until two in the morning sometimes."

The auburn-haired woman purses her lips and looks away. The other keeps still and silent. The brunette speaks softly as she fidgets with the strings of her pouch.

"Sorry, sir."

"Don't apologize to me," Asher replies. "I'm not the one you hurt. That would be Ms. Cleary here—a newcomer, a colleague, a woman striving to make a difference in the corporate world just like you. Now, I won't make you apologize to her, because you're not children, but let me make it clear that I will not tolerate anyone spreading malicious rumors about Ms. Cleary. Is that understood?"

"Yes, sir," all three murmur with lowered heads.

Asher said they're not children, but right now they remind me of three little girls who just got caught making another girl cry in the playground.

And by the cool, cute older boy whom they happen to have a small crush on, no less. They look on the verge of tears themselves and I almost want to hug them and tell them it's alright.

Almost. I'm not that kind.

Asher turns to me. "Ms. Cleary?"

"Yes?" I meet his gaze.

"If you're done with your lunch break, there's something I'd like to go over with you."

"Yes, sir," I answer.

I follow Asher to his office. Once we're inside, I close the door behind me.

"You didn't have to do that," I tell him.

"I did. If the people working for this company turn on each other, we will lose money."

He's right, of course. Still...

"I had it under control."

"Maybe, but..." He stops as he meets my gaze. His eyebrows furrow. "Have I... offended you?"

"No," I answer promptly.

Do I look offended?

"I just..."

I draw a deep breath.

Just spit it out, Violet. Say what's on your mind like that woman did. Ask the questions that need asking. Then you won't have to keep wondering or feel like you're suffocating.

"Mr. Hawthorne…"

"Yes?"

"Why are you being kind to me?"

Asher doesn't answer at once. For another moment, his eyebrows remain creased. Then they arch.

"Oh. Is that what you think of what I just did? An act of kindness?"

Now I'm the one who's confused. Wasn't it?

"It's not just what you did. I'm talking about everything. The coffee. The compliments. All the help with work."

He touches his chin as he leans on the edge of his desk. "I see. You think I'm being kind. That's why you asked me earlier if there was anything I wanted."

I nod.

"You think I'm being kind because I want you to sleep with me?" Asher asks me outright.

I shrug. "I think you're being kind because you need... something. I just can't figure out what."

"Well, I don't," he says. "I have many ways of seducing women. Kindness isn't one of them."

Okay. So I'm right. Asher no longer wants to sleep with me. That's a good thing, right? That's what I wanted? Why then don't I feel relieved?

"Like I said earlier, I'm not expecting anything from you, Ms. Cleary," Asher adds. "So you don't have to worry."

No. I'm not worried. I'm disappointed, hurt. When someone doesn't expect anything from you, doesn't that mean they've given up on you? That they no longer care about you? So Asher no longer cares about me?

I was complaining about being a charity case but I'm not even that. It's like Asher just had this kindness to throw around and I just happened to be there so I got a sprinkle of it.

"Just so you know, I wasn't being kind, Ms. Cleary. I was just being your boss. A nice boss, which is really what I usually am. In fact, if you ask some of the people here, they'll tell you I'm nicer than my brothers."

Right. Asher's just being... Asher. He wasn't going out of his way to be nice to me. He wasn't treating me like I was special. He wasn't being anything, least of all kind, which is cruel, really. I can't stand it.

"Well, you don't have to be," I tell him.

He gives me a puzzled look. "I don't have to be your boss? Ms. Cleary, are you quitting?"

"You don't have to be nice," I explain.

"Like I said, I'm not trying to be nice to you or anything. I'm just—"

"Just don't, Asher." I put my hands up. "Whatever it is, whatever's been going on, just stop it. Don't bring me coffee. Don't send me home early. Don't tell me my dress is nice. Don't ask me how I'm feeling. Don't talk to me."

I put my hands down and draw a deep breath.

"Just leave me alone, Mr. Hawthorne. Please?"

For a moment, Asher just looks at me. Then he shrugs. "Fine."

Fine? That's all he has to say after everything I said?

I turn around and leave.

Fine.

CHAPTER NINE

Asher

"You don't look fine," Glenn tells me as he serves up my second martini. "Tough week at work?"

"Women," I answer before taking a sip.

One woman, to be precise. Violet Cleary.

She's perplexing. I flirt with her. She thinks I'm a jerk. I apologize to her and she still thinks I'm a jerk. I act like a jerk. She won't go away. I give her a present. She introduces my balls to her knee. Ouch. I let that go. I'm practically a saint. I even do nice things for her like I normally do for my best employees. And what does she do? She looks at me like I'm the scum of the earth and tells me to leave her alone.

No. She's not perplexing. Perplexing I can take. I love it even. When I see a math problem that challenges me, I immerse myself in it. I take time to figure out the answer, and when I do, I feel immense satisfaction, like everything in the universe makes sense.

Violet is impossible. She's a problem without a right answer.

"Why is it that women don't make any sense?" I ask Glenn. "You're mean to them and they get hurt. You're nice to them and they still cry foul. They hate you either way and yet they still stick around."

"Women," Glenn mutters as he shakes his head.

"Yup. That sounds like them," Ethan agrees.

I look at him and snort. "You have no right to complain. You have Stella."

"And sometimes I still don't understand her," Ethan says. "The other day, she wanted to have guacamole with chocolate syrup."

Glenn chuckles. "Think women are bad? Pregnant women are worse. They're cranky and whiny. They're roller coasters. One day they're so happy they want to buy every pair of baby shoes in the store. The next they're crying because they can't decide whether they want pink or red nail polish. One moment they're all over you and won't let you leave their side. The next they literally throw up at the sight of you."

"I didn't know you were married, Glenn," Ryker says.

I didn't either, but I don't think he was making any of that stuff up.

I give Ethan a pat on the shoulder. "It looks like you're in for a hell of a ride, big brother."

He frowns. "Thanks, Glenn."

"And don't even get me started about women in labor," Glenn says. "They're the most unreasonable kind."

Ryker shrugs. "I think anyone would be unreasonable if they're pushing a little human out through their—"

"Okay. That's enough," Ethan cuts him off.

"I agree," I say as I try to push the image out of my mind. "You know what? How about we not talk about women while we drink?"

"You started it," Ryker points out.

"And you have no right to complain about not being able to talk about women since you don't have any to talk about," I tell him as I lift my glass to my lips. "Unless you've decided to make a move on your best friend's cute sister."

"What best friend's sister?" Ethan asks.

"Claire Parker," Ryker answers. "Joel's sister. And no, I am not making a move on her or whatever it is your festering mind thinks I should do."

I make a face at his choice of adjective. "'Festering', is it? I really wonder why you haven't found yourself a girlfriend when you're obviously such a cunning linguist."

"You know, that right there pretty much proves my point," Ryker responds.

"I don't mind," Ethan breaks in. "The new rule about not talking about women, I mean. But I thought you wanted to know all about what's going on between me and Stella."

"That was when the two of you had an exciting relationship," I tell him. "Now, the two of you just have sex all the time, which is boring."

Ethan grins. "Trust me. It never is."

"And something I'd rather not have an image of in my head," I add.

"Same here," Ryker seconds.

"Fine." Ethan sets his glass down. "No talking about women, though I doubt you'll be able to follow that rule."

"He won't," Ryker agrees. "The only way Asher will stop talking about women is if he stays away from them, and that's one thing he'll never do, no matter how much women drive him crazy." He looks at me. "Who's the one who doesn't make sense now?"

I take a sip of my martini instead of answering. Ryker's right. I'm not right in the head, either. As frustrating as Violet is—and she's the most frustrating person I've ever met in my life—what's even more frustrating is that I'm still attracted to her. I told myself I would stop caring about her and yet I still do. She's a problem without an answer and yet I still can't help wanting to figure her out.

I guess we're both impossible.

"I'll stop talking about women as long as Ethan shows up every Friday night like he used to," I say before popping an olive into my mouth.

"You know I can't make any promises," Ethan says.

Glenn shakes his head. "His life isn't his own anymore, boys."

Poor Ethan.

I let out a sigh before finishing my last olive. "Fine." I signal to Glenn to make me another one.

Ethan asks for another glass of whiskey as well. "By the way," he says. "How's your apartment?"

I narrow my eyes at him. "I thought we weren't going to talk about women."

"I asked about your apartment."

Yeah, right.

"What's wrong with his apartment?" Ryker asks.

I guess he still doesn't know Violet and I are neighbors.

"Nothing," I answer. "I was thinking about moving somewhere else, but I do like The Mistral. Maybe you should move in."

"And be your neighbor?" Ryker shakes his head. "No way."

I give him a puzzled look. Why not? It's not like I have a pet skunk or throw orgies every night.

That threesome last week doesn't count as an orgy, does it?

"You grew up in the room next to mine," I remind him.

Which means he was my first neighbor. Ethan was in the room at the end of the hall.

"Exactly," Ryker says. "I've had enough of living next to you."

I snort. This brat.

"Besides, I like my apartment," he adds. "Not too big. Not too small."

"Oh, are we making dick jokes now?" I tease him. "Because I thought we weren't drunk enough for that yet."

Ryker frowns. "Well, some of us aren't."

"So you're staying in your apartment?" Ethan asks me.

"Yes," I answer.

I was there first. There's no reason why I should leave.

"Happy now?" I ask him.

Before Ethan can answer, his phone rings. He takes it out of his pocket.

"I thought no phones," I say.

He ignores me and answers the call. A second later, he leaves the stool beside me and heads out to the balcony.

"That must be Stella," Ryker says what I'm thinking.

I turn my attention back to my drink. "So he shows up but he'd rather be at home with her."

"Just be grateful he did show up. Isn't that what you wanted?"

I wanted things to go back to the way they were, but I guess that's not an option anymore.

I drink. Ryker takes out his phone.

For a moment, I consider reprimanding him, but I decide not to. Ethan's already on the phone. Ryker's always on his phone lately. Maybe we should just do away with that rule.

"How are the preparations for Joel's wedding going?" I ask him instead.

"Okay," Ryker answers. "I think. I'm his best man, not his wedding planner."

Right. I go back to drowning my thoughts in alcohol only to have them interrupted when a woman occupies Ethan's seat. I move my glass away from my lips.

"I'm sorry, miss, but—"

The rest of my sentence vanishes as I find myself staring at a familiar face. Painfully familiar. I may have lost count of how many women I've slept with and forgotten most of their names, but I'll never forget the name of the first woman I slept with.

"Farrah West," I say it as I put my glass down. "I must say I never thought I'd see you again."

What was that quote from Casablanca? 'Of all the bars in the world, she had to walk into mine' or something like that. Fate can be mischievous, indeed.

"Asher." She gives me a tentative smile as she fidgets with the heart-shaped pendant of her necklace. "How are you?"

I look away. "You can drop the niceties. I know you're not nice."

I finish my drink.

"I was actually hoping I'd never see you again."

After everything she did to me, I thought I would hit her for sure the next time we met. Strangely, right now, I don't feel angry, just a little annoyed.

I signal to Glenn to pour me another martini before eating my olives.

"By the way, that seat is taken," I tell her.

"Right." She vacates it. "I was just going to order drinks and go back to the table I'm sharing with my husband. He's here on business and—"

"I'm not interested, Farrah," I cut her off.

She nods. "Right."

She walks off, but then she returns to my side. I see the anxious expression on her face reflected on my empty glass.

I glance over my shoulder. "What?"

Why can't women just leave me in peace?

She draws a deep breath. "I know this is probably too little too late to undo any damage I've done, but I just wanted to say I'm sorry for what I did seventeen years ago. I was a child."

"So was I."

I was only sixteen.

"I've spent a long time regretting it," she adds.

I look into her brown eyes. I try to remember what I used to see in them all those times we had sex, before everything turned into a mess. I can't. All I can remember is the hatred that burned in them when she tried to drag me to hell.

"You're right," I tell her. "It's too little too late."

I turn my head away and pick up my next martini. As I drink, Farrah remains standing behind me. What? Is she not yet done? What is she waiting for?

Finally, she leaves.

"Who was that?" Ryker asks as soon as she's gone.

I don't answer.

Moments later, Ethan comes back to his seat. He glances over his shoulder.

"Who were you talking to?"

I set my glass down and snarl, "I thought we weren't talking about women."

And I'm glad I made that rule, because right now, I don't feel like talking about Farrah or Violet, the only two women who've managed to drive me mad. In fact, I want to forget about them both and just enjoy what's left of my evening if at all possible.

I let out a sigh before picking up my glass again.

Women.

CHAPTER TEN

Violet

"Men," I grumble as I pop another piece of popcorn into my mouth.

I couldn't sleep so I decided to watch a movie. To save time, I just closed my eyes and picked one randomly from my list, which is how I ended up with Ever After.

Right now, it's at that scene where the Prince is all alone on a balcony staring at the pouring rain, feeling dejected after Danielle left the ball in tears.

Correction. After he sent her away from the ball in tears.

He could have taken her side. He could have kept her from leaving. Instead, he cast her aside. One minute, he was so madly in love with her that he was willing to endanger foreign relations, and the next he wanted to swat her like a fly.

Why? What is it with men that they can change their minds so easily? They say women change their minds as frequently as they change clothes. Maybe that's true when it comes to what they want to eat, their taste in fashion, what color they want the new sheets to be. But when it comes to feelings, women don't turn them off as easily. When they have a crush on someone, they have that crush for a long time. When they fall in love, they cling to love for as long as they can, even after the other person no longer cares about them. At least, that's what I've observed.

Maybe it's not so much changing minds as having a change of heart.

Whatever it is, it seems it doesn't take much to make a man turn cold. In the Prince's case, he can probably be forgiven because he was deceived. But Asher? What did I do to him to make him stop caring?

I leave my hand inside the bowl as I pause to recall how I've treated Asher in the past few weeks. I was cold to him when I first arrived at the airport. I refused his apology. I threw his present back at him. I kicked him in the balls.

Okay, fine. Maybe Asher has a reason to hate me. I can understand that. What I can't understand is why I care so much about Asher not caring about me anymore.

I grab a handful of popcorn and try to shove it into my mouth. One of the pieces falls on my chest.

I shouldn't care so much. Really, I shouldn't. It's best for both of us if he acts like any other boss and treats me just like any other employee. I can focus on my work. I can climb up the corporate ladder my own way. I don't have to deal with spite from other people at the office. And then outside the office, we can just ignore each other even if we bump into each other in the elevator here at The Mistral or happen to be in the gym at the same time. We'll act like complete strangers. He has his own life that has nothing to do with me. I have mine.

At least, I should have my own life. Maybe that's the problem. Maybe the reason why I care so much about what Asher thinks and feels is because I don't have a lot of other stuff going on. I don't have much that I care about. And maybe I should. Instead of caring about Asher, I should care more about myself, do something for myself.

I glance at the shoe rack in the corner.

I didn't bring a lot of my shoes with me from Switzerland, but I did keep my neon orange pumps.

My clubbing shoes. The sight of them makes me grin.

I wonder what's a nice club I can hit tomorrow night.

~

Well, this seems nice, I think as I step inside Xatharsis.

It took me only a few minutes to find it online. After looking at photos and reading several posts—I found out it got a recent makeover which made it more upscale and more popular—I thought I'd give it a try. So here I am in a glittering little black dress and my shiny neon orange pumps, which I suppose looks good since I got picked out of the line.

So far, I like what I see.

I like the space. I like that it's not too crowded. I like the music, which isn't all volume. I like the hexagonal DJ booth suspended from the ceiling right above the bar in the middle of the room. I like how the VIP lounges look like box seats in a theater but more modern, like they've been cut into the wall instead of protruding outward, more like real boxes. I wonder what it's like to be there but at the same time, I don't. I'm just here to drink, dance and have fun. In that order.

I walk over to the bar, sit on a velvet-covered stool and order an Old-Fashioned.

"Nice shoes," the man seated next to me remarks.

I take a moment to appraise him. Young. Twenty-five maybe. Sandy blond. Lean. Clean-shaven. Nice nose. Cool bomber jacket. Not bad.

I'm not here to flirt, but I don't think there's any harm in flashing him a smile.

"Thanks."

"Nice dress, too, actually," he adds.

What next? Nice clutch? Nice watch? Nice hair?

"You here alone?" he asks.

"No," I lie.

"Oh." I hear the disappointment in his voice. "Right. I'm waiting for my friends, too."

I didn't say I was. And I didn't ask. Maybe I shouldn't have given him that smile.

He offers his hand. "I'm Jake."

I don't take it. Instead, I grab the drink that the bartender set down in front of me, gulp it down and pay.

"I'm going to dance."

I disappear into the crowd on the dance floor and start moving to the rhythm. I don't consider myself a particularly good dancer. I don't dance in front of people or anything like that. But in places like this, no one cares. Everyone's just losing themselves to the music.

That's what I do. I close my eyes and let the music take control. My body moves on its own, my feet stepping forward and back, sliding to and fro, my hips swaying, my shoulders rolling, my head rocking back and forth. I can feel my blood pumping as sweat coats my skin, the endorphins flowing.

Now, this is fun. Definitely much more fun than sitting on my couch watching movies or lying in bed unable to sleep because of Asher.

Asher who? Right now, I don't care about him one bit. He doesn't exist. Tonight on this dance floor, it's just me and this fucking amazing music.

I dance some more until my legs start to feel tired and my throat feels dry. That's my cue to get my second drink. I head to the bar, but as I make my way through the crowd, I bump into a wall.

A wall with blond hair and a bomber jacket.

Jake.

"Hey," I say, though I'm not sure he can hear me. "I was just about to go to—"

"Let's dance," he says.

Then he grabs my wrist and pulls me back into the crowd.

What the hell? I try to pull my arm away but his grip stays firm. I try to shout at him to let me go but he doesn't hear it. Either the music is too loud or he's just pretending not to. At any rate, I can't seem to escape, so I just tag along until he finally stops. He turns around, lets my hand go and starts to dance. I don't.

"What the hell is wrong with you?" I scold him with my hands on my hips.

"What's wrong with you?" he throws the question back at me as he tries to grind against me. "Why aren't you dancing?"

I smell the alcohol on his breath and grimace as I step back.

Don't tell me he went on a drinking spree since I left him at the bar. Brandy, from the smell of it.

Not nice.

When he tries to rub his body against mine again, I push him away with enough force that he nearly stumbles back. Then I bolt. To my dismay, he grabs my elbow. I roll my eyes.

You have got to be kidding me.

My first time at a club in Chicago and I catch the attention of a drunken loser. Great. And I was having so much fun, too.

I try to shake his hand off but it's no use. Should I just kick him in the balls?

I try the diplomatic route first. "Listen, Jake. If you don't let me go right now, I'll—"

"Let her go."

In spite of the loud music gushing out of the speakers all over the club, I hear the deep, familiar voice. I turn my head and my heart stops.

Asher is standing there, the threat clearer in his narrowed onyx eyes than in his voice. His fingers wrap around Jake's arm, which suddenly looks like it might snap in two.

Scary. I've seen Asher angry before, but never like this. He may seem perfectly calm, but I can feel the rage coming off him in waves. The destructive intent. The power. A lump forms in my throat and I swallow.

Jake, too, looks suddenly afraid. He lets me go, his hand shaking as he looks at Asher with wide eyes. As soon as Asher drops his arm, he runs off like a dog with its tail between its legs. I wouldn't be surprised if he's heading to the bathroom before he pees in his pants.

Serves him right.

I turn to Asher, who's still standing beside me. "Thanks."

"You're welcome," he answers, the rage in his eyes gone.

In fact, he's back to the Asher I know, though maybe more like the Asher I first met in the café back at Wharton. Cool. Casual. He's wearing a denim shirt, rolled up to his elbows with the top three buttons undone, and a pair of darker jeans.

Hot.

He looks like he's waiting for me to say something, but I struggle to come up with it.

I've already thanked him. What more do I say? What more does he want me to say?

"I'll just go," he says when the silence has gone on for too long.

He turns to leave.

"Wait." The word just slips past my lips.

He turns back to face me. Like before, he waits, an expectant look in his eyes.

I draw a breath. "Let's dance."

I don't know why I said that, especially when they're the very words that disgusted me so much when Jake said them to me just moments ago. Besides, I was going to take a break from dancing. I'm supposed to be headed to the bar for a drink. Strangely, though, I suddenly no longer feel thirsty or tired.

For a moment, Asher just looks at me. I start to wonder if maybe he thinks I've gone mad. Then he starts to move, to dance. I begin to dance as well, but it's not the same as what I was doing earlier. This time, I can barely feel my body move or hear the music. I can barely feel anything. Everything is a blur, like an image that's still loading. Everything seems unreal.

I still can't believe Asher is here. What is he doing here? I didn't even peg him for the clubbing type, though I suppose clubs must be a good place for him to pick up women. But why here? Why tonight? Is he here every Saturday night? He doesn't own this club, does he?

It's bewildering enough that we're in the same club on the same night. It's even more baffling that we bumped into each other in spite of this crowd.

Bump into each other? No. That's not right. He found me. How? Did he see me from his VIP box? No way. Sure, he must have a view of the dance floor from there, but he couldn't have recognized me, not in this crowd and with this lack of lighting. How did he?

And why did he help me? I thought he didn't care about me anymore. He didn't have to. I had everything under control. Yet he appeared out of nowhere and stepped in. He looked like he was ready to kill Jake, too. That's not what someone who doesn't care would do.

Maybe that's why all of my annoyance with him suddenly vanished—because I realized he still cares. And I'm grateful for it, more than for the fact that he scared Jake away. That's why I asked him to dance.

Or is all that an excuse and I just wanted to dance with him?

"Hasn't anyone told you you're not supposed to be thinking while you're dancing?" Asher asks.

He's right. I'm thinking too much, which is why I'm not dancing like I should. That's not right. If I'm dancing with Asher, I might as well do it properly. Besides, didn't I say I'm here to have fun? Sure, something unpleasant just happened, but surely I can still have some fun before this night is over.

I shove my thoughts aside, tell myself to relax and try to move more freely. Eventually, I hear the music again. I let it seep into my body as I surrender.

Just dance, Violet.

I get so lost in the music that I forget I'm no longer dancing alone. I only remember it when I catch a whiff of cologne and my arm brushes against Asher's.

I open my eyes and find him dancing behind me, our bodies nearly touching. Without thinking, I lean back against him. My back collides with his chest. He leans forward and our bodies rub against each other, moving in sync to the rhythm of the music. My pulse quickens.

Dancing with someone else is so different from dancing alone. And so much more exciting.

With my mind emptied, my senses are more acute. I can smell Asher's cologne and the scent of his sweat. I can feel his breath next to my ear. I can feel the rippling muscles of his chest pressed against my back. He places his hands on my hips and I feel the heat of his palms through my dress. His fingertips send a current buzzing through my veins.

I suddenly become aware of the fact that his crotch is just there behind me. If I grind my hips against him, if he rubs against me with just enough force, I'll probably feel his cock through the layers of clothing separating us, especially if he's getting hard.

Is he?

The temptation to grind is too much, so I have to turn to face Asher. I must have done it too quickly, though, because I nearly lose my balance. My hands land on Asher's chest as I keep myself from falling, and as a result I see the bare, sweat-covered skin peeking from the unbuttoned part of his shirt. My breath catches.

I get an urge to run a finger down the trail of hair running down the middle of his chest. I look away, but then my gaze meets Asher's. His dark eyes look straight at me. Piercing. Smoldering. My chest burns. I can't breathe.

As I part my lips to take a gulp of air, Asher's mouth descends on mine. His hand grips my arm as his tongue slips in. Its tip brushes against mine and I shiver.

His tongue caresses mine as he rubs my shoulder. Heat travels under my skin. His other hand rests on my lower back and another shiver goes down my spine.

He pulls me closer and deepens the kiss even more. His tongue pushes against my palate. A moan vibrates in my throat.

For a moment, I forget that we're in a club, that there are other people watching, that I'm not supposed to be kissing Asher, but as I pull away to breathe, I open my eyes and the spell breaks.

Now I know how Danielle felt when her wing was ripped off the back of her gown.

Just like she did, I run. I make my way through the crowd towards the exit, my heart pounding every step of the way. My thoughts, which were being kept at bay, break through the gates like a flood and churn. One question keeps repeating inside my head.

What have I done?

CHAPTER ELEVEN

Asher

"Where have you been?"

The raven-haired woman whose name I can't remember gives me a puzzled look as I reenter my VIP box.

She's still here?

"Dancing," I answer before sitting down and pouring myself a glass of gin.

I need something bitter to wash away the bitter taste still lingering in my mouth from the fiery kiss I shared with Violet, something strong to dispel the frustration still simmering in my veins.

I lift the glass to my lips and gulp its contents down.

I can't believe Violet bolted. Again. And there I was hoping that the third time would be the charm. In fact, for a moment, I thought we'd finally be going all the way. She was responding even more than before. She was even the first one who leaned against me. She was the one who turned. She was the one who asked me to dance. But just like before, she was just leading me on. She took me to a new height only to drop me and watch me shatter from the fall.

I set down my empty glass and let out a groan.

I guess I should be grateful she didn't shove her knee into my crotch this time, though that doesn't change the fact that my balls were still left a little blue.

"You look upset." My female companion sits beside me and puts her hand on my thigh. Her fingers skitter across the dark denim as she purrs, "Would you like me to cheer you up?"

Would I? I consider her offer for a moment. There's nothing I'd like more than to have sex right now. Rough sex to exorcise the lust still burning in my blood. And this woman is practically begging for it.

But no. Violet was the one who ignited this fire in my loins. She's the only one who can extinguish it. No other woman will do.

I don't want any other woman.

I stand up. "I'm going home."

She gives me a look of disappointment. "Already? But..."

"You can stay until the club closes," I tell her. "I booked this box for the whole night. Feel free to order more drinks and put them on my tab. Just make sure you have someone to call to take you home."

"Sure you don't want to take me home?" she asks with a grin as she plays with a tendril of her hair.

I don't answer. I just grab my jacket and leave. I came here to relax and that's impossible now, so there's no point in staying. I might as well just go home and get some sleep. In my bed. In my apartment next to Violet's.

I frown. On second thought, maybe I'll just stay at a hotel until Monday.

~

Come Monday I've put the whole incident behind me. Or so I think until I see Violet in my office. One look at her and I remember Saturday night. I remember how she looked in that little black dress. I remember rescuing her from that jerk. I remember the dance. I remember the kiss.

And, of course, I remember her running off like Cinderella at the stroke of midnight, which I'd rather not.

This is why I wish we didn't have to work together.

Judging from her expression, Violet seems to remember everything, too, but she pulls her shoulders back and puts on a smile.

So she's going to pretend nothing happened, is she?

"I just wanted to ask you what you thought of the report I gave you last Friday, if you've had a chance to look at it."

"I have."

She rubs one of her fingers. "And?"

I hear the expectation in her voice, so I narrow my eyes at her.

"Ms. Cleary, are you fishing for a compliment? Because I seem to remember you specifically telling me not to give you any."

I'm not surprised. Like I said, Violet may be smart, but she doesn't seem to know what she wants.

"I'm not asking for a compliment," Violet replies. "Just feedback."

"It's fine," I tell her as I lean back in my chair. "For future reference, if you don't hear anything from me, your report is fine. If it isn't, you'll know. Loud and clear."

Violet doesn't seem to be happy with that.

She draws a breath. "About the things I said last Friday..."

"Let me guess. You didn't mean them."

Her eyebrows arch. "Well, I... I meant it when I said you didn't have to be nice to me and bring me coffee or anything like that."

"You said you didn't want me to be nice to you," I correct her.

There's a difference.

"Anyway, I didn't mean that we should stop working together."

"You said you didn't want any help with work, either."

"But I'd still like us to work together," she says. "To communicate about work."

"That would be helping you with work, wouldn't it?"

"No. That would be you being my boss."

"Being a nice boss, which you were against."

Violet sighs. "So what? You're going to be the mean boss again?"

"Do you want me to be?" I ask her.

She doesn't answer. I shake my head and grin.

Violet frowns. "Is something amusing?"

"You, Ms. Cleary," I tell her.

Her eyebrows furrow. "Me?"

"Yes. You being so smart and independent and yet having no idea what you want, especially from men."

She says nothing.

"But you know what's not amusing? Other people suffering because of your indecisiveness. Like your boss who doesn't know what to do with you because you don't like him yelling at you or buying you coffee."

"That's..."

"Or the man you danced with at that club and kissed passionately and then abandoned like a shoe that no longer fit."

There. I've said it. I wasn't really planning on bringing it up, but I guess I just can't keep it in any longer.

Regardless of whether Violet is being a cocktease on purpose or just plain indecisive, what she's doing is wrong. It's about time she got a scolding.

And she does look like a child that's just been scolded. Guilty. Penitent. She's not going to cry, is she? Because this time, I'm not going to let her off easy even if she does. Tears are for babies. When you're a grown-up and you've done something wrong, you try to make it right.

She can't keep going like this. She has to make up her mind.

She draws another deep breath. "I'm sorry... for leaving you at the club like that."

I say nothing because an apology isn't enough. There has to be more.

"If you want to go back to yelling at me again, that's fine. I'll live with it."

I shake my head. "No."

Violet's eyebrows arch.

"I'm not going to decide what to do next," I explain to her. "In fact, I'm not going to do anything. You decide, Violet. If you don't want anything to do with me, all you have to do is stay away from me. Move out of The Mistral. Find another job. Go back to Switzerland and you'll never have to see me again. But if you do want me the same way I want you—and I think you do—you know where to find me. I won't ask you any questions. I won't expect anything. I'll just be waiting. But not forever. God knows I've been patient long enough."

For a moment, Violet stays still, silent. Then she parts her lips as if to say something, but no words come out. She closes her mouth again as she fidgets with the hem of her blouse.

Now, she really looks at a loss.

I clear my throat. "You can go now, Ms. Cleary."

She leaves, but I can sense her confusion lingering in the air. Well, that's not my problem. It's hers. She's the only one who can sort out her own feelings.

The ball is in her court now. All I have to do is sit here and wait for her to make her move.

I tap my fingers on my desk.

What are you going to do, Violet?

CHAPTER TWELVE

Violet

I don't know what to do.

It's been three days since I had that conversation with Asher and I still haven't made up my mind, which basically means I've been living in hell these past few days.

I can't sleep. I can't focus. Whenever I'm sitting down, I find myself adrift. It doesn't matter whether I'm watching TV at home, at a meeting here at work, or behind my desk trying to read something on my computer screen. Or eating. My mind just escapes from me to go on its own quest and my body goes on autopilot, like sleepwalking except you're awake.

In fact, that's what just happened. Right now, I have half a turkey sandwich in my hand and I can't even remember eating the other half. My mouth just bites and chews. I can't even taste the turkey. I don't remember the taste of the quiche I had for breakfast either.

I set down the remaining half of my sandwich on my plate with a frown. I think I've just lost my appetite.

This is hell, alright. Then again, maybe not. When you're in hell, at least you know you're doomed. There's nothing more you can do but suffer the consequences of your actions, your choices. I haven't done anything yet. I haven't made my choice. So I'm in limbo. I'm still waiting for my judgment, judgment that I have to pass on myself.

I have the power to choose between heaven and hell, except my choices aren't that clear cut. If they were, I wouldn't still be torturing myself. My choices are to leave Asher and never look back—or stay and give in to what he wants, what he says we both want. Basically, it's have sex with Asher or leave.

I don't want to leave. I've already fallen in love with Chicago. I've already grown used to my new job. So what then? Do I just have sex with Asher and stay?

It sounds so simple, but it's not. I don't take sex lightly. I don't just do it with anyone. And I think Asher knows that. That's why he wants me to be the one to come to him. Well, that and the fact that the past few times he's tried to get close to me, I've pushed him away.

If I'm the one who approaches him, I can't push him away. I have to be all in, which is exactly what Asher wants. He thinks it's what I want as well, but is it?

Do I want to have sex with Asher Hawthorne?

"Hey." A voice breaks into my thoughts, forcing my mind to go back into my body.

I nearly jump. No one's ever approached me in the office cafeteria before. And I definitely wasn't expecting anyone to.

I turn my head to see who it could be and find a familiar-looking petite brunette. Now, where have I seen her before?

Oh, right. She's the one from outside the bathroom, one of the friends of that auburn-haired woman who tried to pick a fight with me.

"I'm Michelle," she introduces herself with a smile, a real one this time. "Mind if I sit?"

She doesn't seem to have any evil intentions, plus she's carrying a full tray of food that she looks like she might drop at any moment, so I nod.

As she puts her things down, I wonder what she might want from me. There must be something or she wouldn't be sitting with me. As I glance around, I notice there are plenty of free tables and seats.

This is on purpose. The question is: What's her purpose? Is she here to apologize? But she didn't have to sit with me to do that. Is she going to offer to be my friend because maybe she's realized I don't have any and the ones she has aren't so good? Or is she just here to talk to me about makeup? Or maybe ask me about work?

"You're Violet, right? I think that's a nice name. It's my favorite color, actually."

She shows me her purple nail polish.

"I see."

So she's here to show off her nails?

"I'm so sorry about what Linda did. Linda, she's the woman who said nasty things to you."

I guess it's option one, then—she's here to apologize on behalf of her friend. The question is: Should I accept her apology?

"I hope you'll forgive her," she goes on. "Asher Hawthorne is like a hero to her. She nearly got fired once when she was going through her divorce. It was Mr. Hawthorne who let her stay.”

“Really?”

I guess Asher is a nice boss.

“But of course it’s up to you if you want to forgive her. You’re not obliged. I actually hate it when people say sorry and then get mad at you when you don’t forgive them. I won’t. Get mad, I mean. I’m not forcing you to forgive her. I was just trying to explain why she acted that way. And no, she didn’t send me to make excuses for her or ask me to apologize for her. I just thought I would since, well, she does owe you an apology and she knows it but she’s a little scared to talk to you.”

Which makes Michelle a good friend, though maybe one who talks too much.

“She’s scared?” I ask.

She didn’t seem scared when she was talking to me.

“Believe it or not, it took Linda a lot of courage to say the things she did,” Michelle says.

Which I actually kind of admire, especially now that I know how hard it is to be honest.

Honest? Wait a sec. Doesn't honesty require that you already know something? But I don't know what I want yet. Or do I and I'm just refusing to admit it, just like Linda knows she owes me an apology but won't give me one because she's scared of me?

I've always been the kind of person to know what I want. I know myself well, which means I already know whether or not I want to sleep with Asher. I know. I'm just having a hard time accepting it because I'm dishonest.

Or scared. More of scared.

"Violet?" Michelle's voice pulls me back to earth again.

"Sorry," I mumble. "You can tell Linda it's fine. I forgive her."

Michelle's eyes grow wide. "Really?"

I nod. She was only being honest, after all. Besides, I'm not one to hold grudges.

Except the ones against the two men who broke my heart.

"By the way, I really do love your lipstick," Michelle says.

I take the tube out from my purse and hand it to her so she can take a look at it.

"That's what I use. I bought it in Paris."

"Paris?" Her eyes grow wide again. "You've been to Paris?"

"A few times."

It was only four hours from Zurich by train, after all.

"Wow." Michelle hands me the lipstick back. "Now I really want to be your friend."

She does? Come to think of it, I could use a friend. Maybe if I had someone to share my mind with, it wouldn't drift off so often.

"I'm a really good friend," Michelle assures me. "I'll even share my dessert with you."

She pushes her slice of chocolate cake towards me.

I lift my hand. "No, thanks. I actually don't like chocolate that much. I probably had too much of it when I was in Switzerland."

"Too much? Wow. I've never heard of anyone who's had too much chocolate."

I have. During my first few months in Zurich, I tried every chocolate shop and bought every piece of chocolate available. Once, I even bought three boxes and finished them all in one sitting.

"You can have my juice instead." Michelle offers me the unopened bottle.

I shake my head. "It's fine. I have my water anyway."

I take a sip from my bottle. She frowns.

I guess she really wants to give me something. She doesn't have to, though. She can still be my friend.

I'm about to tell her that but she speaks first.

"Ask me anything, then."

What?

"Ask me anything," she repeats with an eager grin.

Okay. I draw a deep breath.

"If someone broke your heart once and you didn't expect to see him again but you do and now he wants to have sex with you, would you say yes?"

Michelle's eyebrows arch. "Whoa. I wasn't expecting that."

And I realize I've just said too much.

"It's okay," I tell her. "You can just forget..."

"Let's see." She touches her chin as her eyebrows crease. "How did he break your heart? Did he cheat on you?"

"Something like that."

"Jerk. And how long ago was this?"

"A long time ago."

"And now he wants to have sex with you? Like he told you he wants to have sex with you?"

I wish she wouldn't keep saying 'sex'. I know I said it first, but somehow it sounds weirder when she says it. And louder.

I glance around before answering. It's a good thing there aren't too many people around and no one nearby.

"Basically."

Michelle nods. "Okay. So let me ask you this. Do you want to have sex with him?"

I look at her. Wow. She really gets straight to the point, doesn't she?

I don't answer. I think I know the answer, but I'm not ready to tell anyone yet.

"I'm not asking if you want to get back together with him. That's not what he's asking, right? I'm just asking if you want to have sex with the guy? Yes or no?"

I let out a breath and scratch the back of my head. Fine. I have to be honest at some point.

"Yes. But…"

"But you're afraid he might take it as a sign that you've forgiven him. You're afraid that he might think you want to get back together. Or that you might want to get back together because you might realize you're still in love with him."

Wow. Michelle really speaks her mind. In a lot of words. But I can't really deny what she said.

Except the last part. I can't still be in love with Asher because I was never in love with him. He didn't give me a chance to be.

I can fall for him for sure this time, which I guess is what I don't want to happen. What I'm afraid might happen. I don't want to take the first step to my downfall.

Michelle grabs my hand. "You're afraid because you think you're not in control. But you can be. You can have sex with him and then decide, dictate even, that it's just sex. It doesn't have to mean anything, but in case it does end up meaning something, then you can decide whether to accept it or just forget about it. You can give him a second chance or you can walk away. You make that call, and whatever call you make, it's okay."

She does make sense, so much that I'm amazed. How can a person you've never talked to before put your thoughts and feelings into words when you've been struggling to do it for days? How is it that I didn't know what to do but Michelle does?

"You know what I think?" Michelle asks.

"I'm listening."

"I think you're too serious, too hard on yourself. You think too much. Unnecessarily."

True.

"If you want to do something, just do it. If it turns out to be good, be happy. If it turns out to be bad, walk away from it. Regret it if you must, but forgive yourself. Move on. Go do something else that you want."

That simple, huh? Or maybe I've just really been overcomplicating things.

Michelle squeezes my hand. "Go and get some of that sex your sleazy ex owes you. For yourself. Not for him. We all need it every once in a while."

She's right. I haven't had sex in a while. Maybe that's why I had an orgasm while imagining Asher's hands on me. Maybe that's why I leaned against Asher on the dance floor. Maybe that's why I kissed him back with tongue. That... and if I'm being completely honest, the fact that I was a little upset that Asher and I didn't have sex in the gazebo that night.

I need to quench this thirst for sex and this curiosity about Asher, and it seems that Asher needs to quench his desire for me. Who knows? Maybe after we both fulfill each other's needs, we can get over each other, move on from the past and just get along at work. Or maybe I'll decide to leave and never look back.

At any rate, it will just be sex. No strings attached. No feelings. It will be just like a cleansing ritual, like how two people who resent each other yell at each other to feel better. But instead of yelling, we'll be having sex.

It might just be the best thing for me and Asher.

Michelle sighs as she lets go of my hand. "I guess this means you and Asher Hawthorne really aren't a thing."

I pause. She was talking like she knew me so well that I almost forgot she didn't know about me and Asher. I wonder how she'd react if she knew I was talking about him. But I guess there are things that are better kept even from your friends.

"No," I tell her. "We aren't."

We'll just have sex once and that's it.

Michelle pouts. "Pity. If Asher Hawthorne asked me to have sex with him, I'd definitely say yes."

I grin. That's exactly what I'm going to do.

~

When I arrive at my apartment after work, I head straight to the shower to shave my legs. And my pubic hair. Then I shower. With a new floral-scented body wash. Thoroughly. Afterwards, I blow my hair dry and put on the lace panties and the satin chemise I just bought. I spray on a bit of my favorite perfume as well. Then I don my robe. The only problem I have is what shoes will go with it.

Should I just wear my bedroom slippers? Or do I put on my heels?

I opt for the latter and head down the hall. I take a few moments in front of the door to Asher's apartment to gather my composure and mentally rehearse what I'm going to do.

Okay. So I'm going to ring the doorbell. Then when Asher opens the door, I'm going to give him a grin and pull on the sash of my robe so he can see what I'm wearing underneath. Hopefully, that will reveal my intentions without me having to say a single word and he'll pull me into his arms and kiss me. If not, I'll just kiss him first. And then we'll take things from there.

I close my eyes and draw a deep breath. I can hear the alarm blaring inside my head telling me to back off while I have the chance, but I ignore it. I've already made up my mind about what I'm about to do, and this time, I'm going all the way.

I'm going to have sex with Asher.

I'm still scared, yes, but I'm also excited and looking forward to finally getting this over and done with. I've waited long enough.

I lift my hand to press the button for the doorbell. It rings. I feel a little disappointed when no one answers immediately, but I simply ring again. I hear footsteps coming from inside the apartment and my heart starts to pound. My fingers tremble slightly as they grip the sash of my robe.

Here we go.

I hear the door lock come undone and I hold my breath. The door opens and my heart stops.

It's not Asher standing in the doorway but a woman with olive skin and long, coral red hair like a mermaid's. Her eyelids are painted emerald, the same shade as the deceptively transparent lace dress clinging to her slender body.

For a moment, she stares at me with narrowed eyes like I'm a pest. Her full, scarlet lips form a pout. Then she slams the door in my face, so loud I barely hear my hopes and plans for the evening shattering in the aftermath.

I guess I'm not having sex with Asher tonight.

CHAPTER THIRTEEN

Asher

I thought Violet and I would have had sex by now.

These past few days, I've caught glimpses of her agonizing over the decision I asked her to make. Each time, I felt a combination of annoyance and pity. I wanted to just go over to her and put her out of her misery, out of both our miseries. But no. She has to be the one to make the move. I know what I want. She has to do the same.

Yesterday, when our eyes met and I saw a gleam in them I'd never seen before, when the corner of her mouth twitched ever so slightly, I thought she was finally ready to give in. I thought tonight would be our night.

Instead, today, she's more hostile than ever, which is a pity because she looks so hot in her red dress. Each time our eyes have met, she's either rolled her eyes or glared at me. Once, she even cursed under her breath. And not the 'I'm screwed' kind of curse but the 'I don't deserve this' kind, which makes me think I've done something to offend her.

At this meeting, she's been nothing but rude. She tried to interrupt me or contradict me at least a dozen times during the first few minutes. Then she just stopped listening whenever I talked and didn't even bother to hide it. Obviously, she's mad at me. Everyone in the room can see it. The question is: Why?

What did I do?

I decide to ask her after the meeting. As her boss, I can't tolerate this kind of behavior. As someone waiting for her to make up her mind whether she hates me or wants me, I'm concerned. Either way, I have to know the reason for her tantrum.

As soon as the meeting is over, Violet tries to leave ahead of the rest of the people in the room. I stop her before she reaches the door.

"Ms. Cleary?"

Her shoulders sink as she stops in her tracks.

"You and I still have a few things to discuss."

"Fine," she mutters.

She stomps back to the table and drops into the chair furthest away from mine, closest to the door.

She crosses her arms beneath her breasts. Her lips are glued into a pout. Somehow, she reminds me of a kid who hasn't been allowed to leave the dinner table to go play because she hasn't finished her vegetables.

I wait for the other people who were at the meeting to leave the conference room. Then I close the door and lock it. I don't plan on letting Violet out until I get to the bottom of this newfound resentment, and I don't want anyone to interrupt us while I'm interrogating her.

I lean against the long table, leaving an empty chair between Violet and me to give her some space. I grip the edge and clear my throat.

"Is this PMS or something else?"

"PMS," Violet answers.

Yeah right.

"Liar," I scoff.

"Excuse me? Did you just call me a—?"

"Liar," I repeat as I look at her. "We both know something's going on with you."

Her eyes throw daggers at me. "Yes. You would know, wouldn't you?"

I wish I did. Then we wouldn't be having this conversation, which I have a feeling is about to turn into a fight.

"Actually, I don't," I confess. "I know you're pissed at me about something, but—"

"Pissed?" Violet interrupts me. "If a man missed his train to work, he'd be pissed. If a student left his homework at home, he'd be pissed. This is more than that."

"Fine. Enraged. Infuriated. Homicidal. That doesn't change the fact that I don't know why."

Violet's eyebrows go up. "Excuse me?"

I put a hand on my hip as I turn to face her. "What did I do, Violet?"

For a moment, she just looks at me. Then she claps her hands above her head.

"And the Oscar goes to... Asher Hawthorne, ladies and gentlemen!"

My eyebrows furrow. "You think I'm acting?"

She puts down her hands and looks at me.

"You really don't know, do you?"

"No."

Violet purses her lips and shakes her head.

"Tell me," I urge her.

"She didn't tell you? She thought I was too insignificant for her to talk to you about, didn't she?"

She?

"I don't know who you're talking about," I tell her.

"Right. Because you have too many women that you can't keep track of them all. Maybe you should have your own app made just for that."

Now I don't know what she's talking about.

"Anyway, it's not them I'm mad at. They all probably just got tricked. They got seduced, had dirty things whispered in their ears and were promised all sorts of stuff..."

"I never promised them anything."

"They got fooled into thinking sex with you was the best thing that could happen to them, that it was something they wanted, needed." Violet shakes her head. "Well, you can't fool me."

So she's decided not to sleep with me. Pity. I was hoping she'd go the other way. Still, I respect her decision.

I let out a breath. "If you didn't want to have sex with me, you could have just said so in the first place. There's no need for all this drama…"

"Drama?" Violet stands up and slams her hands on the table. "You think I'm just trying to put on a show for you?"

I think I can't take this much longer.

Violet puts her hand on her chest. "You hurt me, Asher. Again. See. This is why I don't go near you. Because every time I do, each time I give you just a slight opening, you stick a spear into my heart."

"Again, I don't understand what you mean. I didn't do anything. You're the one who's rejecting me. You're the one who just crushed my hopes after raising them."

"Really? I broke your heart? That's not possible. You don't have one."

"Neither do you," I tell her.

She wants to be brutally honest? Fine. I'll be honest with her. And brutal.

Violet points a finger at me. "Don't you dare put me in the same boat as you. You… you're a monster."

I cross my arms over my chest and grin. "Is that the best you can do?"

"You're a man-whore," she tells me next.

Ah. More insulting.

"And you're a cocktease," I tell her. "And a drama queen."

She sneers. "You're a man-child."

"Surely I can't be a child and a whore at the same time."

"You're everything vile."

"Now that's just vague."

"You tell a woman you want to have sex with her so she shaves and goes to your apartment in freshly bought lingerie only to have another woman who looks like a cross between a Victoria's Secret model and Aquaman's wife open the door and slam it in her face."

That's specific. Is that what happened? Violet came to my apartment and saw another woman there? I think I know exactly who.

Hold on. Violet came to my apartment. That means...

"What are you grinning for?" she asks me. "It's creepy."

I keep doing it anyway. "Now I know what you're talking about."

She gives me a puzzled look. "What?"

She thought she knew what was going on, but she doesn't. I do. The tables have turned.

"I finally understand everything," I tell her. "You don't."

"Excuse me?"

"The woman you saw at my apartment, the woman you thought I was sleeping with—her name is Roxanne Garcia."

"I don't care who she is."

"She's my house manager," I inform her anyway because she has to know. "That means she hires the people who clean and maintain my apartment and makes sure they do their jobs. She makes sure my laundry's done, the linens are changed, the pantry is stocked…"

"I know what a house manager is," Violet cuts me off.

And judging from the blush on her cheeks, she's aware that she misunderstood the whole situation. Yup. She's been spending the whole day getting mad at me for no reason. I think she owes me an apology.

I don't hear one. Instead, she sinks into her chair, puts her elbows on the table and mumbles, "House manager."

"Yes. House manager."

I rest my arm on the back of the empty chair next to the one she's sitting on as I move closer to her.

"She's had the job for about two years now. The one before her was an older woman. Jane. I fired her when I caught her sleeping with the plumber in my bed."

Violet doesn't seem to be listening. She takes a few strands of her hair and presses them between her nose and her lips as she stares blankly at the table. Then she lets them go as she turns her head to meet my gaze.

"House manager?"

"Yes. I swear I've never slept with her." I look into her blue eyes as I lean on the edge of the table. "And I haven't slept with anyone since the last time you showed up in front of my apartment."

Something flickers in her eyes. Surprise? Joy?

That disappears as they narrow. "And you think I'd believe you?"

"You should," I tell her. "Because I'm telling you the truth."

"So what? I'm just supposed to take off my clothes and have sex with you now?" she asks.

"Sounds good."

Violet snorts. "Sorry but I don't sleep with men who have house managers."

Oh. She's back to insulting me? Yet I can tell that unlike earlier, there isn't any venom in her words this time.

I hold her gaze as I lean forward. "Stuck-up."

"Man-child."

"Drama queen."

"Pompous ass."

I lower my face so that it's almost level with hers. "You shaved."

She pauses a moment before answering. "I shaved."

Which means she wants to have sex with me. And so do I. Right now.

I press my palm against Violet's cheek and place my lips on hers. I apply just a slight amount of pressure at first, just enough for me to feel our lips touching. Then I push harder, smearing her lipstick. I part my lips and let just the tip of my tongue out to taste it as it runs across her upper lip. Then I take her lower lip and suck on it gently.

Violet's hand goes over mine. For a moment, I stop, afraid that she might pull my hand away, slap me and walk off. Instead, she strokes my hand as her lips press firmly against mine. My heart leaps. My cock throbs.

I continue to kiss her, and more passionately. Now that I know Violet wants this, I'm not holding back. Over and over, our lips collide in perfect synchronization. My hand slides to her jaw, hers to my shoulder.

She clutches my shoulder as she gets out of her chair to stand in front of me. I straighten up, grip her hip and plant a long kiss on her lips. When she parts them, I push my tongue inside her mouth. She trembles. Her arm goes around me.

She caresses my back as my tongue caresses hers. My hand travels up and down the side of her dress. When my fingers brush against the curve of her breast, she moans. The sound sends ripples of heat beneath my skin all the way to my crotch.

I don't find a zipper on the side of her dress so I search for it on the back. I find it. As I pull it down, Violet pulls my shirt out of my pants and starts to unbutton it from the bottom. She manages to undo just three before I take over. She steps back to slip out of her dress and her shoes. I discard my shirt and my tie.

I start to unfasten my belt but Violet wraps her arms around my neck and kisses me. My fingers fumble as I kiss her back, worse when she rubs her breasts against my bare chest. Even through the lace, I can feel her pert nipples poking my skin, and it causes my cock to poke the front of my boxers. I nearly groan.

Come on.

Eventually, I manage to get my belt free of its buckle. I pop the button of my pants and pull the zipper down just to give my erection a bit of breathing room. Then I focus all my attention on Violet.

I grip her hips and perch her on the edge of the table. My fingers wade through her sea of curls as I kiss her. Then I pull her head back gently so I can plant my lips on her neck. My other hand cups her breast through her bra.

I rub her nipple through the lace and she gasps. Her nails dig into the back of my shoulder. I unhook her bra and she takes it off. I trap one of her nipples between my lips and give it a playful twist. She moans.

I circle her nipple with the tip of my tongue as I slip my hand past the garter of her panties. The first thing I realize is that she has indeed shaved, which sends a buzz through my veins. The second thing is that she's wet. Soaking wet. My cock swells.

She's even wetter inside, I learn as I push my finger in. And warmer. And fucking tight. Is she a virgin? I thought she said she wasn't. At any rate, I can barely slip one finger in, so I don't try another. I tease her nub instead.

Violet's arms fall off my shoulders as she lets out a soft cry. She leans back on them, trembling, gasping as I continue to tease her. Her hips jerk. Eventually, her upper body falls on top of the table, her arms limp at her sides.

Surrender. This is what I've been waiting for.

My heart pounds in my chest as I conquer her mouth. My tongue pins hers down as two of my fingers try to enter her. This time, they slide in with ease. I move them in a scissoring motion to stretch her and then push in deeply. Violet pulls her mouth away from mine and gasps.

She closes her eyes and turns her head to the side so I lick her ear as I bury my fingers in her heat. My cock complains in my boxers. I continue to ignore it and begin to move my fingers. When Violet's hips start to move to meet my thrusts, I know she's ready.

And I definitely am.

I pull her underwear off as fast as I can. Then I pull my boxers down to free my stiff, aching cock. I take the condom out from my wallet and slip the rubber sheath over my cock. Afterwards, I position the tip right next to her shaved, glistening wet pussy lips. I rub it against her for a few seconds before gripping her thigh and pushing it in. I hear another loud gasp in response.

The passage is still tight but my cock manages to slip inside Violet's body inch by inch. Halfway in, I shift my gaze to her face. Her eyes are still closed, squeezed shut now. Her whole face looks flushed, her features tense. Her lips are parted but no sounds escape.

I don't ever want to forget this look on Violet's face as I enter her.

I stroke her cheek and she opens her eyes halfway. Pleasure swims in her sapphire eyes. My breath catches.

I don't ever want to forget this look, either.

I lean over and kiss her. My lips remain on hers as I continue to enter her slowly. When I can't go any further, I pause. I pull my mouth away and stare at her face as I start to jerk my hips.

Violet places her hands on my shoulders. I move faster and her nails dig into my skin. Her eyes close. Her mouth gapes open as she gasps for air in between soft cries.

I grip her hips and give one hard thrust. My cock fills her to the hilt and she lets out a sharp cry as she wraps her arms around me. I find it hard to move with her clinging to me so I lift her upper body and pull her hips against me. Her legs wrap around my waist.

I continue moving, savoring the friction between our bodies. It's better than I ever imagined, so good I know I won't be able to last much longer. Judging from the sounds Violet is making and the way she's clinging to me, neither can she.

I grab her feet from behind me and put her heels in my hands. I rock her body back and forth on my cock so I can bring her over the edge first. Sure enough, she starts to tremble. Her body arches as she throws her head back and lets out a cry.

"Fuck!"

As she starts to tighten around me, I grip her hips once more and thrust my cock inside her. I only manage a few thrusts before my balls start to feel hot and heavy and my muscles start to coil. I clench my jaw and let out a few grunts as I bury myself deep inside her and release all of my pent-up desire.

I wait until she's milked me of every drop and I've regained enough air in my lungs. Then I pull out. I leave Violet for a minute to dispose of the used condom in the trashcan, making sure it's buried under scraps of paper. When I turn towards her again, she's sitting in a chair, putting her panties back on.

Why is it that I find even that sexy?

I fasten my belt as I watch her put on her bra and then her dress. She seems to be having a hard time with the zipper so I help her.

"Thanks," she mumbles.

I realize it's the first thing she's said in the past several minutes—well, not counting the curse that escaped her lips when she reached the climax of pleasure. I feel like I should say something, too. But what? I normally don't have conversations after sex. I just put on my clothes and leave.

Before I can say a word, Violet leaves the room without so much as a backward glance. I frown.

I'm glad we had sex. I'm glad Violet didn't run away in the middle of it. And yet, for some reason, I don't feel as satisfied as I normally do, which is strange because I did enjoy every second of it.

I run my fingers through my hair and scratch the nape of my neck.

What the hell is wrong with me?

CHAPTER FOURTEEN

Violet

I can't believe I did everything wrong.

I had a plan for the first time I had sex with Asher. I was going to be in lingerie, fresh from a shower. We were going to do it in his apartment. Afterwards, I was going to tell him that it was never happening again, that it didn't mean anything and that the two of us should move on and try not to be a pain in each other's asses any longer.

Instead, I made a grave mistake in assuming his house manager was his lover—seriously, what was I thinking?—we had sex in the conference room at the office—unbelievable—and then worst of all, I forgot to talk to Asher afterwards to clear things up.

Actually, I didn't forget to. While I was putting my clothes back on, I felt like I had to say something to fill the awkward silence. I knew I was supposed to say something. What I forgot was what I was supposed to say. I just couldn't remember any of it. Maybe it was because I was tired. Maybe it was because I was shocked that I just had sex in a conference room. Or maybe it was because my head was still spinning from that sex, that fucking amazing sex that I'd dreamed of for years. At any rate, my mind went blank, or more accurately, stayed blank—because let's face it, my coherent thought processes turned off way before that—so I didn't get to say anything.

Now that I'm home in my apartment and I've had a shower and dinner, my mind is clear. I remember what I wanted to say and I realize I still have to say it. I have to wrap things up neatly. Years ago, Asher and I didn't have any closure. We just went out and then we didn't go home together and we just stopped talking to each other. Maybe that's why I haven't completely been able to get over him. This time, we have to talk. I have to tell him that it's over.

My mind made up, I grab my cardigan and head next door. No need to put on lingerie. I'm just going to talk. I ring the doorbell twice. No one answers. I ring it a third time. Still nothing.

I step back to check if there's light beneath the door. There is. I press my ear against it but don't hear a sound.

Maybe Asher's not here. Maybe he left the lights on or they're automated, but he's not here. It's Friday night, after all. Asher could still be at the office finishing work, or at the club. Or at a hotel sleeping with another woman, which for some reason makes me furious. How can he have sex with another woman just hours after he did it with me?

I shake off the feeling and the idea. No need to jump to any conclusions. Look what happened last time. All I know is that Asher isn't home, so I just have to come back tomorrow and tell him everything I need to then. Plain and simple.

~

Not that simple.

Now that I'm here standing in front of Asher, who's wearing just a robe and looks like he just woke up, I can't seem to find my words again.

Instead, all I can think of is how good he looks with his hair uncombed. Some of the strands tumble over his forehead and I can't help but want to brush them off with my fingers. I can't help but stare at the hair on his chest, exposed between the flaps of his robe, and wonder if he's wearing anything underneath it. Boxers? Briefs? Somehow, I can't remember what he had on when we had sex. I can't remember what his cock looks like either, which is weird because it was inside me. I'm pretty sure I saw it.

I glance at Asher's crotch.

How can you have sex with a man and not remember what his cock looks like?

"Violet?"

I pull my gaze up to the level of his eyes and try not to blush. I try, but I fail when I see Asher grinning like he knows what I was just thinking.

Damn it.

"I..." I touch the side of my neck and clear my throat. "I hope I didn't wake you."

"You didn't."

"Good."

I fold my arms beneath my breasts and draw a deep breath.

Focus, Violet.

"I came by last night," I tell him. "But you didn't seem to be home."

Asher's bushy eyebrows arch. "You did? Well, I hope no woman answered the door this time. Otherwise, I might have to call the police."

"No." I shake my head. "No one answered."

He leans on the door frame. "By the way, I told Roxanne that you were my neighbor, so next time, she shouldn't slam the door in your face."

He did?

I put my hand on the nape of my neck. "You didn't have to."

"No, I think I did. She was rude to you because she thought you were one of those women trying to get inside my apartment to steal my stuff."

My eyebrows furrow. "There are women like that?"

"Yeah. You know, women who say they've left their panties behind but they really want to get a pair of my boxers as a souvenir."

So he wears boxers. That doesn't mean he's wearing a pair right now, though.

"That's creepy," I say, trying to stick to the topic at hand.

"Yeah. Also, once, there was this woman who bugged Roxanne to let her in so she could wait for me in my bed. In handcuffs."

Handcuffs? Is Asher into that? I wouldn't put it past him. In fact, if I remember that week when he was bringing women home every night, it seemed like he was into everything. It sounded like it. Me? I've never experienced being tied up, but I can't say I'm not curious. Too bad Asher and I will never get to try it.

Whoa. Did I just think I wouldn't mind having sex with Asher again?

"Anyway, Roxanne has had some bad experiences with women showing up at my door so... that's how she reacted. But she knows better now. She knows you're not like those other women."

I'm not? For some reason, hearing that sends a thrill down my spine.

"So you came to my apartment last night?" Asher asks me as he scratches the back of his head.

"Yes," I answer.

"I'm sorry I wasn't here. I was with my brothers."

"Really?" That didn't even cross my mind.

"Well, brother. I was with Ryker. Ethan couldn't make it. Lately, he's been... busy. But we're supposed to have a thing every Friday night."

"Oh. That's nice."

I thought they weren't that close, since even though they work at the same company, in the same building, they barely seem to talk to each other unless they're in a meeting. I didn't think they saw each other during the weekends either. I just thought they'd be too tired and busy with their own personal lives. It's nice to know I was wrong, that the bond between Asher and his brothers is still strong, just like what I caught a glimpse of back in Zurich. Of course, the fact that Ethan has been busy is unfortunate, but I guess it's inevitable that would happen sometimes. And at least they do have a brotherly ritual.

"Anyway, did you need something?" Asher asks. "Did you want something... from me?"

His ebony eyes narrow. My breath catches.

"Did you maybe forget to say something? Or do something?"

I know I forgot to say something, but now I'm starting to think it's more of the latter. There are things I could have seen, things I could have done, things Asher could have done to me. After all, as incredible as the sex was, it happened so fast. It started and ended so fast.

It ended too soon.

"Or maybe there's something more you want from me?"

More? Yes, I definitely want more. Yesterday wasn't enough. It was sudden and rushed and in a conference room. Besides, I never said I was only going to have sex with Asher once. All I said was that it would just be sex. And it will still just be sex no matter how many times we do it.

I want more.

I clutch the front of Asher's robe and push him back, crossing the threshold of his apartment. Then I lean forward to kiss him.

He closes the door behind me and I find my back against it as his mouth crushes mine. Over and over.

This part I remember. After all, we've already kissed three times before. Or is it four? All I know is that by now, I've memorized the shape of Asher's lips and how firm yet soft and smooth they feel against mine. But that doesn't mean I've grown bored with Asher's kisses. Or that they no longer have any effect on me.

As he sucks on my lower lip, I can feel the back of my legs tingle. His tongue brushes against mine and I shiver.

Asher's kisses still make me weak. I love them. All I'm saying is that I want to experience other things with Asher, too. Things I've never experienced before.

I push off his robe and let my fingers travel over the chiseled, hardened muscles of his broad chest and his rigid abdomen. I can almost feel them getting giddy from mapping the amazing terrain. My fingertips brush against the soft curls in the middle of his chest and I follow where they lead, all the way down to the garter of his underwear.

So he is wearing underwear. I try to find out what it is without looking, my fingers running over the cotton. They graze against a wet spot and Asher breaks the kiss to suck in a breath. I give him a mischievous grin as I press the palm of my hand against the front of his boxers—yes, I think they're boxers. The bulge swells and a sound rumbles deep in Asher's throat.

See. This is something I didn't get to try last time, which is a pity because I find it fun.

I kiss Asher as I start to move my hand slowly. Even through the cotton, which seems to be getting damper, I can feel the heat from Asher's cock. I can feel the shape of it. The thickness. I can feel it throb.

I start to move my hand faster but Asher grabs my wrist. I open my mouth to complain but then I meet his gaze. His dark eyes look straight into mine, soft yet also intense. They command me to be silent and I purse my lips. He brushes his against them as he takes my other wrist.

He leads me to the bedroom and pulls my shirt off my head. I suddenly wish I had worn a better bra. Asher doesn't seem to mind this one, though. He plants a kiss on the valley between my breasts and then sucks my breast through my bra as he unbuttons my shorts and pushes them down. They fall to my feet and I step out of them.

Asher pushes me down on the bed. As soon as my back hits the mattress, his mouth is on mine. I run my hands over his back and my fingers through his hair. His hands go over my shoulders, my arms, my sides, my hips, my thighs. Everywhere they touch, my skin comes alive.

I'm coming to life. A while ago I was drowning in Asher's kisses, and now I'm basking in the sun, in the warmth from his skillful hands.

He reaches behind me to unhook my bra. I slip the straps off my arms. He takes one of my breasts in his mouth and I gasp. He sucks and I moan.

He plays with both my nipples, one with his tongue and the other with his fingers. My arms fall at my sides as I tremble. My hands clutch the sheets. The ache between my legs grows.

When it becomes too much to bear, I grab Asher's wrist and put his hand there. He lifts his head and grins.

"Impatient, aren't we?"

I reply by reaching for his crotch. I wrap my fingers around the bulge there, which seems to have grown bigger since the last time I checked. He grunts.

I flash him a grin of my own. "So it seems."

Asher takes my hand and licks my palm. It tickles so I suck in a breath.

"Don't worry," he tells me. "I'll give you as much attention as you want."

He pulls my panties off and settles between my legs. The next thing I know, he's parting my other pair of lips. His tongue slides in between.

My hips jerk. A moan escapes my lips.

He continues to lick me and I start to tremble. My nails dig into the mattress. Each time his tongue enters me, heat floods my belly and spreads through my veins. My mind gets lost in a haze.

When his thumb presses against my nub, my hips jerk again. My moans spill into the air as the pleasure from both his tongue and his fingers drives me crazy. I fight it at first because I'm afraid it might be too much, but eventually all I can do is surrender. As soon as I do, waves of heat roll over my skin. I grab Asher's hair and try to hold on as my body arches. My toes curl. My eyes roll to the back of my head.

"Holy... fuck..."

The curse slips past my lips just before I run out of breath, of speech, of thought. For a moment after, my mind drifts off. My body goes numb. Then the sound of a drawer opening jolts me back to reality.

I turn my head to find Asher standing by the bed. He takes out a packet of condoms from the drawer, then pulls his cock out of his boxers. My eyes grow wide as I finally lay eyes on it. Just as I thought, it's thick. And long. Massive. I feel a tinge of fear at the thought of that entering me, but at the same time I can't help but feel excited.

The place he teased tingles. I'm ready for more.

I watch Asher as he slips the rubber sheath onto his cock. Even if I wanted to tear my gaze away, I couldn't. I'm mesmerized.

When Asher turns, our eyes meet. His lips curve into a grin.

"Ready?" he asks.

I respond by stretching my arms out to him eagerly. He just brought me to a cloud of pleasure and I'm still on it. I want him to join me there as well.

He climbs back on the bed and kneels between my legs. Then he grabs a pillow which he slips beneath my butt to lift my hips. He grips my thighs and I brace myself for what's to come.

Like before, I feel a slight discomfort as his cock enters me, stretching me. But it fades. The more he fills me, the more excitement swirls in my veins. I feel like I'm on a roller coaster. Right now, the car is still climbing slowly up the rails, trudging along, but I know it will soon reach the top and then...

I let out a cry as Asher gives a hard thrust that reaches deep inside me. And then everything just speeds up. I grip the edges of the pillow under me as I scream and gasp.

"Oh God! Oh God! It's so... good!"

Asher pounds into me.

"You like that?" he asks after a particularly hard thrust.

I do, but it's not enough.

"More," I tell him. "Faster."

He complies. The bed creaks. My head spins. My vision starts to blur.

Asher grabs my ankles as his pace becomes erratic. Then he buries himself deep inside me in a final thrust. That thrust sends me over the edge, causing me to tremble as I push my hips against Asher, trying to take him even deeper. As deep as I can. My cries mingle with his grunts. Then we both fall silent as we gasp for air.

It's over.

I let go of the pillow and lie still, too tired to move. When Asher pulls out, I just let my legs fall on the bed. After a few seconds, I pull the pillow out from under me and hug it to my chest as I lie on my side.

Now what? Am I satisfied now? Is this enough?

Something inside me tells me no. But what if it is enough for Asher? What if he tells me to leave his apartment?

I'm about to sit up, but then I feel Asher's arm around me. He's lying behind me. His breath tickles my ear. His erection pokes my back.

Erection?

He brushes my hair aside and kisses the nape of my neck. Then he whispers in my ear.

"I've got nothing else to do this morning. What about you?"

I turn my head to meet his gaze. "Nothing."

He grasps my chin. "Then would you like to stay a little longer?"

My lips curve into a grin. "Sure."

~

That sure was… incredible to say the least, I think as I wipe the cum off my chest in Asher's bathroom. That's the result of me asking him to do me raw, which was probably the best time we did it.

I glance at my reflection in the mirror and smile.

How many times did we do it? Three? Four? I can't even remember how many orgasms I had. But I do know that I've just had the best sex of my life. And now I'm worried that it may never happen again.

Is this it? Is this the end?

I linger in the bathroom because I'm afraid to find out, but I can't stay in here forever. Finally, I draw a deep breath and step out. I see Asher already in his robe and my heart sinks.

I guess it really is over.

"Water?" He offers me a bottle.

I pick my panties off the floor. "I think I'll get dressed first."

"Okay."

I gather the rest of my clothes and head back to the bathroom.

"But before you do…"

I stop in my tracks.

"Have you been around Chicago since you came here? What have you seen?"

I look over my shoulder. "Not much. Why?"

He gives me a charming, boyish grin. "Would you like to go to the Navy Pier with me tonight?"

CHAPTER FIFTEEN

Asher

The Navy Pier—my favorite place in all of Chicago.

I can still remember the first time I came here. That was at night, too. My mother had just been buried and I was grieving. I don't know why. I didn't even get to know her that well or spend much time with her. But I was lonely. One of the maids took pity on me and whisked me out of the house without my father knowing. She brought me here, thinking it would cheer me up. It did.

And it still makes me smile.

Maybe it's simply because of the bright, colorful lights that are reflected on the water and illuminate the sky. They remind me of the Northern Lights I saw in Finland once. Maybe it's because of the music, the sounds, the bustle—they're all proof that life goes on. Maybe it's because of the majestic view of the city. Or the serenity of the lake, undisturbed by all that's going on. Or maybe it's the happy faces of families and couples. At any rate, whenever I'm here, I seem to forget whatever it is I'm missing—a mother, a higher purpose, friends, love. It's my happy place.

I think Violet likes it, too. She seems to be taking in all the sights with the wide eyes of a child in awe. And she's smiling, which brings a glow to her cheeks and coats her eyes with a gleam so that she looks stunning even in a simple cream-colored cardigan over a pink turtleneck and light denim pants.

I should have known she'd look good in anything. After all, she looks good even in nothing.

The image of Violet's flushed, naked body on top of my bed revisits my mind. I banish it. For now, I want to soak in every second of my time with a clothed Violet.

"Do you like the place?" I ask her just to be sure.

She nods. "Yeah. From here, Chicago looks a bit like Zurich."

Does it? Now that I think about it, I realize she's right. They're both on a lake, after all.

"So I guess your record stays perfect," Violet says.

"Record?"

She looks at me. "Isn't that why you brought me here? Because all the girls you brought here before liked it here?"

So she still thinks I'm a man-whore? Ouch.

Actually, I've never been here with a woman, apart from that maid. I usually bring my dates to hotel bars or restaurants. That way, I can bring them straight up to a room afterwards. Or halfway through.

I guess I have been a man-whore.

Still, Violet is the only woman I've brought out here to the Navy Pier. But I don't tell her that.

"You think I brought you here to impress you?" I shake my head. "Sorry, but I don't do that."

She grins.

"I brought you here because you're going to buy me dinner," I tell her.

Her eyes grow wide. "What? Why would I do that?"

"There's a game here called the Atomic Rush. You go around the maze touching the lights in the color you've chosen. The more you touch, the more points you score. If you somehow get a higher score than me, I'll treat you to dinner. Whatever you want. If my score is higher than yours, you buy me dinner."

"I see." Violet touches her chin. "So this is a challenge, is it?"

"Consider the gauntlet thrown."

She pauses to decide whether or not she should accept it. I know she wants to. She loves challenges. She's just hesitating because she's not sure she can beat me. And it's not because she doesn't have enough money to treat me to dinner. It's a matter of pride. I've never met a woman who hates losing as much as me.

"Don't worry," I tell her. "We'll do a practice round so you can get the hang of it first. Then we'll have three rounds and tally the scores. How about that?"

She looks at me. "That sounds fair."

I thought that would do the trick.

I give her a grin. "So, are you ready to buy me dinner?"

She gives me a grin of her own. "Oh, I'm ready to kick your ass."

~

And she tried. But in the end, I was still quicker, so here we are at my favorite tavern on the Pier with a free slab of barbecue ribs and a can of my favorite lager. Violet ordered the Cobb salad, fries, a slice of key lime pie and a glass of California Chardonnay. In spite of all that, she doesn't look happy.

"Good food, isn't it?" I ask her.

Violet doesn't answer.

"It's even better when you're not eating with a long face."

She lifts her head to meet my gaze, her long face still on.

Okay. So that didn't work. What else can I say to try and cheer her up?

"For your first time, you did good," I tell her.

She pauses in the middle of eating a fry and narrows her eyes at me. "Better than all the other women you've brought here?"

Violet sure is competitive.

"Way better," I answer.

"Liar," she scoffs.

What the hell?

"You're just being nice, which you're not," she says. "You know what else you're not? That good.

You only beat me by twelve points. I'll beat you next time. Also, I tallied my points faster than you did."

That she did, but only because I was distracted… by her. I didn't really have a chance to look at her while we were playing because I had to focus to win. That was how good a fight she put up. When it was finally over, I couldn't help but stare, and so I guess I got distracted.

"You're a sore loser," I tell her.

She looks at me with an angry expression.

Okay. Fine. Maybe I shouldn't have called her that, especially since she probably still is… sore after all the sex we had this morning.

I let out a breath. "Fine. I'll let you ask me a question as a consolation prize. Any question."

Her eyebrows crease. "Just one question?"

"Fine. Three."

That makes her grin. Finally.

She eats a forkful of salad and takes a few seconds to chew.

"Okay. First question."

Here goes.

"What's your favorite movie?"

I nearly laugh. That's it? And here I thought she was going to ask me a serious question.

Still, I decide to take this seriously and answer, "Imitation Game."

Violet nods. "Good choice."

I'm glad she approves.

She takes a sip of wine as she thinks about her next question.

"Would you rather... be able to read minds or be invisible?"

"Hmm." I set my fork down. "This one's tough."

Especially since they're not the super powers I'd really want to have. If I had to choose, my top three would be super strength, invulnerability and flight.

"Read minds," I answer.

Then I could find out who's really on my side and who's not and make sure the latter don't get in my way.

"So you can get any woman to sleep with you?" Violet asks.

Please. I don't need to be a mind reader for that. In fact, if I could read minds, it would be too easy.

"Is that your third question?" I ask her.

Her eyebrows arch. "Oh. No, it's not."

I didn't think so.

"Careful," I say. "You don't want to waste your third question."

Again, she pauses to think. I brace myself.

"Why do you sleep around?" Violet asks.

I wasn't expecting that. And I don't know the answer.

Why indeed? Is it just because of what happened with me and Farrah? Or is it something deeper? Am I damaged? I don't know. I've never been to a shrink.

I shrug. "Because I love sex?"

I thought Violet would blush. She looks pretty when she blushes. Instead, her eyes narrow.

"You don't sound sure."

"Well, it's true," I tell her. "I just don't know if it's good enough for you."

She says nothing and goes on to eat her salad in silence.

Okay. Now I wish I could read her mind.

Have I offended her somehow? Does she hate me more now? Is she never going to have sex with me again?

When Violet showed up at my door, I was genuinely surprised, more so when she started kissing me. I didn't think she'd want to have sex with me again. I didn't think I'd want to have sex with her again. But I did. And so we had sex again and again and again. And still, I want more. Weird.

"Did you sleep with Casey?" she asks me.

My eyebrows furrow. "Who's Casey?"

She sighs. "My friend from Wharton. The one you saw with me at the café. The one you said you'd ask out sometime."

Oh. Her. Honestly, I can barely remember what she looked like.

"No."

"Okay."

She continues to eat her salad in silence. What? Does she not believe me?

I suddenly have an urge to tell her that she's special, that she's unlike all the women I've met. Maybe then she wouldn't look so worried. But if I did, would she believe me?

I decide not to.

"Do you want to walk around after this?" I ask instead before glancing at my watch. "If we finish in half an hour, we can still go to the garden. Then we can go to East End Plaza, which has the best views of the lake. How does that sound?"

Violet doesn't answer at once. During that moment she takes to make up her mind, I worry she might say no. I secretly let out a breath of relief when she nods.

"Yeah. Okay."

I smile. "Great."

Hopefully, all the walking will cheer her up.

~

It did.

At least, I thought it did because Violet was smiling and chatting and taking pictures almost every step of the way. But now that we're on the Centennial Wheel, which I thought was the perfect way to cap our evening, she's back to being quiet again. And unmistakably sad as she looks out of the car.

"Is everything okay?" I can't help but ask.

She turns to me with a forced smile. "Yeah. This night has been fun."

I'm glad to hear that.

She turns her gaze back to the skyline in the distance. "And the views from here are just spectacular."

"They are."

Then why does she look sad?

"I'm fine," Violet tells me. Or is she trying to convince herself? "I just... I don't know... It's... I'm sorry."

"It's okay."

"I thought I would be fine riding a Ferris wheel since it's already been nearly two decades but I guess I'm not," she says. "I..."

Violet draws a deep breath.

"My dad and I used to ride the Ferris wheel every summer, up until he... left."

That's why.

She wipes the corner of her eye then shakes her head. "I'm sorry. I didn't mean to..."

"It's okay," I tell her again. "There's no need to apologize. It's just... We can't just jump off the Ferris wheel."

"I know. I'm fine."

No, she's not.

I take her hand and squeeze it as I look into her eyes. "If only I could fly you away from here."

This is why I'd rather be able to fly than read minds or be invisible—so that I can fly away whenever I want.

"If you could fly, I bet you'd be flying away from me," Violet says. "I'm such a lousy date."

"You're not."

She snorts. "I'm sure none of the women you've brought here before have cried."

I nod. "You're right. That's because I've never brought a woman here before."

I don't know why I said that. Violet's gaze just seemed to pull the words right out of my mouth. And there's more.

"Not on this Centennial Wheel. Not to the Navy Pier, which happens to be one of my favorite places in the world, by the way."

Violet frowns. "I don't believe you."

"It's true. I like Venice, too, and Kyoto and—"

"I mean about you not bringing any woman here before," Violet says.

Oh, that.

I stroke her hand. "Well, it's true whether you believe me or not."

For a moment, she obviously still doesn't, but then I see a glimmer in her blue eyes. A glimmer of faith. Of hope. And of joy.

And desire.

She leans forward. I meet her halfway. Our lips meet for just a few seconds but I feel the heat from it all throughout my body.

I stroke her cheek. "Now I really wish I could fly you away from here."

She gazes straight back at me and grins. "Me too."

CHAPTER SIXTEEN

Violet

As soon as we get inside the elevator, Asher and I continue kissing. After we get off, I lead him down the corridor and we stumble into my apartment, which is closer. We've barely managed to make it through the door when I start taking off his jacket.

I don't even know why we're having sex again. We did it countless times this morning and I'm still a little sore, a little tired. All I know is that I've had the most amazing date and I don't want it to end just yet.

Yes, there were times when it was a letdown, like when I lost to Asher in that maze game or when we started talking about his sleeping habits and when I acted like a fool crying on the Ferris wheel, but overall it's been amazing, incomparably better than the first time Asher asked me out. This is how that date should have ended. This is how this one will.

This time, I get to bring him home to my bed.

I take off Asher's shirt next. He takes off my cardigan and my blouse. Then I get rid of my pants and kick off my shoes while he steps out of his.

Stripped down to our underwear, we head to the bedroom but only make it as far as the kitchen. Asher backs me up against the counter. I feel its cold edge against my waist, just above the garter of my panties.

I grip the edge and lean on it as his tongue melts mine. His hands run across my back and over my breasts, which have started to swell against the padding of my bra. He clutches my ass and gives each soft cheek a firm squeeze before turning me around. I lean on my arms over the counter.

Asher unhooks my bra. As the straps hang from my arms, he puts his hands on my breasts and licks my ear. He plants kisses in my hair and down my back as he plays with my nipples. He traps the stiff peaks between his fingers and twists them or pinches them gently then rubs them. Heat spreads beneath my skin.

He pushes my hair aside and plants his mouth on the nape of my neck. His thumbs slip beneath the garter of my panties and tug them just below my hips, just low enough so he can slip his fingers inside me from behind. They slide in easily.

My body welcomes them, remembering the sensation they gave me just hours before. My mind gives in to the pleasure, knowing resistance is futile. All I can do is try to keep standing as Asher's fingers move inside me. When my knees and elbows start to tremble, I bend forward, leaning on my elbows. My nipples brush against the cold marble. Moans spill from my lips.

Asher's fingers reach in deeply and I let out a soft cry. They press against spots hidden deep inside me, spots that turn me into a mess inside and out. And yet, they feel so good that I can't stop moving my hips against him, wanting those digits even deeper.

No. I want something else even deeper.

When Asher withdraws his fingers, I think I might be getting it. Instead, his arm goes around me. His fingers search for my nub.

I grab his wrist as I straighten up and lean against him. Then I place his fingers where they should be. They start to strum and my body arches. My head crashes against his shoulder.

Asher kisses my neck as he strokes my breast and my sensitive nub. I turn my head and our mouths collide. But then the pleasure from his fingers becomes too much and I have to break the kiss to let out a gasp. I cling to his arms as I try not to collapse on the floor.

His fingers enter me once more and I tremble. He starts to move them in and out of me and I grind against him, wanting more. I feel something hard poke my back and excitement shoots through my veins.

It's exactly what I want.

I turn around and go down on my knees so that my face is at the same level as his crotch. Then I lower his boxers to free his cock. I already saw much of it this morning, but the sight of it hard and leaking still takes my breath away.

I wrap my fingers around the base and press a kiss against the tip. Some of the liquid oozing there ends up on my lips. I leave it there as I brush my lips against the side of his cock, spreading the substance on his skin. Then I clean it up with the tip of my tongue.

Asher's hands land on my shoulders and grip them firmly as a shiver goes through him. He sucks in a deep breath.

I continue to lick his cock all the way to the base. Then I take his balls gently in my hand and press a solemn kiss on the soft skin as if in apology for hurting them before. I still can't believe I did that.

"I'm sorry," I whisper against them before bringing out my tongue.

"It's fine," Asher tells me hoarsely. "Just be… gentle with them from now on."

I try to do that. I try not to apply too much pressure on them with my mouth or with my fingers. I simply cradle them in my palm and plant kisses on them. Then I turn my attention back to his cock. I lick the tip, which sends another shiver through him, then I wrap my lips around it.

I take his cock slowly inside my mouth. I can't take much of it, but what I can I rub with my tongue. I suck and Asher's fingers bite into my skin.

His hands move to my hair as I start to move my head back and forth. His fingers get lost among the curls. I move my head faster and feel the friction build. My lips grow numb from the heat.

Suddenly, Asher holds my head steady and takes over. He jerks his hips, thrusting his cock into my mouth. He shoves it in and I almost gag. Tears bead in the corners of my eyes.

Then he pulls away. I fall back on my heels as I take gulps of air. He grabs my arms and pulls me to my feet.

"I'm sorry." Asher wipes the corners of my eyes. "I shouldn't have done that."

I shake my head. "It's... fine."

I was just surprised, that's all.

Asher strokes my cheeks. As his eyes gaze into mine, I once more find myself unable to breathe. He cups my face and gives me a kiss. It's so tender that my heart skips a beat.

I don't care what just happened. Everything has been perfect. Well, almost. There's one more thing I want. And I know Asher does, too.

He turns me around once more. As he pulls my panties down to my ankles, I bend over the counter again. He kisses the back of my shoulder as he grips my hips. He enters me with a single thrust and I cry out.

He pounds into me and all I can do is cling to the counter for dear life. It's cold and hard but I don't care. There's enough heat in my veins, filling every part of my body. Soon enough, it explodes. My toes curl. A cry rips through my throat as my body quivers.

Asher manages a few more thrusts that rock my trembling body. Then he pulls out and I feel a warm splash on my back as he grunts. More drops follow.

I lie still over the counter until he's done and even after. I just can't seem to move. I think I'm about to fall asleep, in fact, when I feel something coarse against my skin. I realize Asher is wiping my back with a paper towel.

After he cleans me up, he carries me to my bed and tucks me under the covers. Then he starts to leave. Without thinking, I grab his arm. A single word leaves my lips.

"Stay."

For a moment, Asher just looks at me. Then he crawls under the covers beside me and wraps his arm around me. My lips curve into a smile.

As I close my eyes, I can't help but think how good this feels, maybe even better than the sex. And even as the haze of sleep starts to settle inside my head, my mind starts to wonder.

If I had agreed to have sex with Asher back then, would we have ended up like this? Would we have started a relationship, become boyfriend and girlfriend? If I ask Asher if he wants to have a relationship with me now, will he say yes?

CHAPTER SEVENTEEN

Asher

I don't know.

As I have Sunday brunch with Ethan and Stella on the patio, I can't stop thinking about everything that happened between me and Violet yesterday. We had so much fun and the sex was just as mind-blowing for me as it obviously was for her.

I don't remember ever being so happy spending the day with someone, not even with Farrah. And I definitely didn't sleep in her bed. But I did that last night. I slept in Violet's bed. I wasn't planning to, but when she asked me to stay, I just couldn't refuse. I thought I was just going to hold her until she fell asleep, but I ended up falling asleep as well. I only left early this morning when the sun was just starting to peek out.

So what does it mean? Are we going to keep doing this? Do I want to? Does Violet?

I don't know.

"Had a late night?" Ethan asks me as he picks up his cup of coffee. "Let me guess. You were clubbing again."

He probably thinks I had sex in my lounge, too.

"No." I take a big bite out of a roll of bread. "I didn't go to a club. I was at the Navy Pier."

His eyebrows go up. "You were?"

"I love it there," Stella gushes. "Ethan and I went on the Ferris wheel once and the views were just lovely. But I guess I can't go anymore. I have a feeling I might throw up."

Ethan looks at her. "We can go after the baby is born."

Stella beams. "Really? Oh, but do you think they let babies on the Ferris wheel? Do you think it will be safe? Do you think...?"

I stop listening, simply watching their faces and gestures as they talk. They're obviously in love and happy. Well, a little anxious about the future, but also happy. In fact, I've never seen my brother this happy. And Stella's face is simply glowing, which could just be from the pregnancy but I don't think so.

Come to think of it, yesterday, Violet's face was glowing, too. Not just when we were at the Navy Pier but also when she was asking me to stay in her bed. Does that mean she wants to be with me? If I stay with her, can I make her happy?

"By the way," Ethan says to me. "There's a fundraiser in Toronto next weekend. I was going to send Ryker since he likes to go to these things, but he hasn't even returned from the one in Boston last night. Do you want to go? I would but I don't want to leave Stella."

"And I don't think I can ride a plane," Stella says as she touches her stomach.

Toronto?

"Yeah, sure," I answer.

Why not? I don't have plans next weekend and I'm always up for going out of town.

Ethan nods. "Okay. Great."

He starts to nibble on a strip of bacon but Stella nudges his arm.

"Aren't you forgetting something?" she asks.

"Oh, right."

He gobbles up the rest of his bacon and wipes his hands on the table napkin. Then he looks at me.

"The reason why Stella wanted you over for brunch…"

"Just me?" Stella complains.

"Why Stella and I wanted you over for brunch," Ethan corrects himself, "is because we wanted to tell you something."

"Okay." I put my fork down. This seems important.

Ethan looks at Stella and she takes something out of her pocket. A diamond ring.

I give her a puzzled look. "You're not proposing to me, are you?"

Ethan frowns. "Very funny."

Stella laughs. "No, silly. Ethan proposed to me and I accepted."

She slips her ring on.

"We're getting married."

"We are," Ethan confirms.

My eyes grow wide. "Wow."

I know they're in love and they're having a baby, but to think they're serious enough about each other to get married? I mean, marriage is supposed to be a lifelong commitment. No other men or women. No secrets. No lies. No giving up even if you get tired. No turning back.

Is that something I'm capable of?

Frankly, I don't know.

"Congratulations," I tell my brother and his fiancée. "And cheers!"

I raise my cup of coffee.

Stella sends me a smile. "Thank you."

I say nothing more. I don't know what else to say. I'm happy for them, of course, but I also can't help but worry whether Ethan is making the right decision. Then again, maybe it's just me I'm worried about. Now that Ethan is settling down, I'm starting to wonder if I should, too, or if I should at least be more serious about women, maybe start a relationship with one—Violet, to be precise.

Didn't I say something to Ryker about waking up next to her and doing things with her? Didn't I just do that?

But the question is: Can I keep doing it? Because that's what a relationship is about—doing things over and over and still being happy.

Can I do that? Am I ready?

~

I'm still asking myself that question as I stand in front of the door to Violet's apartment. I'm not even sure I want to go in. If I do, won't that mean I want to keep things going with her? Then again, if I don't, I have a feeling everything will end, and while I'm not sure I'm ready to have a serious relationship with Violet, I know for sure I'm not ready to stop having sex with her and just having fun with her.

So I ring the doorbell. I hear her come rushing to the door after the first ring. Moments later, the door opens. Violet appears in a purple tank top, no bra, and gray yoga pants. Her hair is still damp from her bath. I can smell her shampoo.

"Hey," I greet her with a smile.

She looks at me from head to toe and gives me a puzzled look.

"You went out?"

I glance down at my outfit. I guess she would think that since I'm wearing a flannel shirt over a plain white tee and dark jeans.

"Yeah," I answer. "I went to see Ethan."

"Oh." Her furrowed eyebrows straighten out. "Is something wrong?"

"No. Everything's fine. He just... wanted to discuss some things that he didn't have a chance to last Friday."

Violet nods. "I see."

Still, she looks upset. And it seems like she doesn't want to let me inside her apartment. Is it because I left without telling her? But she was asleep. It's not like I waited for her to sleep and then left, even though that was what I was planning.

"Is something wrong?" I decide to ask her outright.

"No," she answers, but she doesn't sound convincing.

I sniff something. "Are those... pancakes?"

"Yeah." Violet glances over her shoulder as she rubs her arm. "I made some for breakfast."

"I see."

She purses her lips for a moment then meets my gaze as she speaks. "There are still a few left over if you want them."

I feel a sense of relief. Violet may be upset with me for leaving, but at least she isn't shutting the door. And now, she's inviting me in.

I smile. "You know I love pancakes."

"Do I?"

She opens the door. I step inside and take a moment to look around since I didn't get a chance to last night. My gaze falls on the marble counter and I smile.

Violet heads behind that counter but I grab her wrist.

"Actually, I'm still full. Ethan made me eat a lot."

"Oh." I hear the tinge of disappointment in her voice.

"But I can eat some later," I tell her.

Her eyebrows furrow. "You're staying? For the day?"

I shrug. "Do you want me to leave?"

"No, but..."

She falls silent as she tugs her hand away. I can see the anxiety on her face as she clutches the front of her top. She draws a deep breath.

"What is this, Asher?"

I know what she's asking. It's the same thing I've been asking myself all morning. And which I still haven't found an answer to.

"What are we doing?" she asks.

I take her hand and brush my lips against her palm. She draws a breath.

"Sex," I answer. "If you want to."

She says nothing.

"Sex that I'm not doing with anyone else," I elaborate.

"So it's just sex?"

"Sex and the Navy Pier and pancakes," I tell her.

I wish I could say more, but right now, it's all I can promise.

"And maybe a movie while we're having leftover pancakes," I add. "And maybe drinks."

Her forehead creases. "Beer and pancakes?"

I shrug. "Why not?"

Again, Violet falls silent. What? Is what I'm offering her not enough for now?

I brush the wisps of hair off her face and stroke her cheek as I look into her eyes.

"And by the way, what we have is not just sex," I tell her. "It's amazing sex."

I place my mouth next to her ear.

"And we haven't even had the best yet."

Violet pulls her head away. "Are you trying to seduce me, Mr. Asher Hawthorne?"

It does seem to be my strong suit.

I rub her shoulder. "Is it working?"

She grins. "Fine. Show me what you got."

So it did work.

I kiss her ear. "Gladly."

I ease my hand up to Violet's neck as I slide my lips across her cheek. I grasp her chin as I press my lips to hers. I suck on her lower lip gently, taking my time kissing her, letting our lips converge over and over as I cradle her jaw in one hand and trace circles on the skin along her hip, just between the hem of her top and the waistband of her pants, with the other.

Violet opens her mouth. I lick her lips first. I drag the tip of my tongue over her upper lip, then the lower. When she sticks her tongue out to meet mine, I take it between my lips and suck. Only after that do I push my tongue inside her mouth. It rubs against hers and she moans. The sound starts a current of excitement through my veins.

I grab the hair at the back of her head and kiss her deeply. My other hand climbs over her tank top to find her breast. I tease her nipple through the cotton as I let my tongue dance with hers.

When she pulls away for air, I lead her to the living room. It's nice to have sex in the kitchen and all, but we've already done that. Besides, I need a place to sit.

I sit on the couch and pull Violet on top of my lap so she's straddling my thighs and facing me. Then I pull off her top. I grip her hips as I worship her breasts one at a time. She grips my shoulders as she trembles. I suck on each mound of flesh and take each peak between my lips. I circle it with the tip of my tongue until it grows as hard as a pebble and then I swipe my tongue against it, over it, again and again. Violet throws her head back and moans.

When I'm done worshiping her breasts, I start a trail of kisses along the inside of her arm. When I get past her elbow, I take her arm so I can plant a kiss on her wrist. After I do that to her left wrist, I pause.

"When did you get this tattoo?" I ask her as I stare at the ink on her skin.

"When I was in college," Violet answers. "You know what it means, don't you?"

I try to decipher the symbols.

"There exists, therefore infinity?" I translate them literally.

"Close," she says. "As long as we exist, there are infinite possibilities."

I give her a grin. "I see."

I kiss her wrist again.

"And that's especially true when it comes to sex."

I push her off me so she's sitting on the couch. I take off her pants and her underwear and kneel on the floor. I pay homage to her long, slender legs by dragging my lips across her skin. When they go over her knee, she stifles a giggle.

"That tickles?" I ask though I already know the answer.

"Yes."

I kiss it some more and lick it until Violet can't hold back her laughter.

"Stop!" She tries to push me away.

I obey. I have other interesting things planned anyway.

I lie on the rug and grab her arm.

"Come here."

I pull her on top of me and guide her hips so that she's straddling my head.

"What are you doing?" she asks with a bit of concern.

"Admiring the view," I answer as I do just that. "And this..."

I clutch her ass as I begin to eat her up. I start from the outside, making sure I thoroughly lick her other pair of lips and tease her nub, which causes her to tremble and gasp above me. Then I push my tongue in and let it play. Violet grabs my hair and lets out soft, incoherent sounds.

I reach up to grab one of her nipples and rub it between my fingers. Violet's back arches before she falls forward, her hands above my head. I grip her hips as I continue to savor my treat. Suddenly, she cries out. Her thighs quiver. Then she goes completely still.

I caress her thighs as I wait for her to catch her breath. When she does, she gets off me and lies down on the rug.

I begin to take off my clothes, starting with my flannel shirt. Violet watches me with eyes sparkling with interest. I'd undress more slowly, but I have a pressing problem in my boxers. A huge problem.

As soon as I'm naked, I sit on the couch and pull Violet back onto my lap. Like before, she faces me and straddles my thighs. This time, though, I guide the tip of my cock inside her as I lower her hips. She sucks in a breath as I enter her, then takes control the rest of the way.

Inch by inch, she takes me in until I'm completely inside her. Even with all the sex we've had, she's still so tight that her velvety skin clings to my cock. Each time she moves, I have to fight the urge not to sheathe myself inside her with just one thrust.

Patience.

Finally, I don't have to. Violet pauses a moment to catch her breath. I let her do that before claiming her mouth in a fiery kiss. Then I press my cheek against hers and whisper in her ear.

"Hold on tight."

I draw a deep breath, place my arms under her legs, clutch her ass and stand up slowly. Violet gasps as she wraps her arms around my neck.

She clings to me as I straighten up, even more when I start to move. This position is strenuous, tiring, but I haven't been working out for nothing. I hold Violet as I jerk my hips and thrust deep inside her. Cries spill from her mouth against my ear.

After a few thrusts, she starts to tremble once more. Her nails dig into my skin. I keep going. Harder. Faster. Too late I realize I didn't put on a condom. Why didn't I? I'm sure I still had one left in my wallet. All I can think of is that I was too excited, too impatient. And I just wanted her to feel really good.

At any rate, like I said, it's too late.

I put every ounce of strength I have left into a final thrust and let myself explode inside Violet's body. Even with my arms trembling, I make it a point not to drop her, but as soon as I'm done, I sit on the couch. I let my arms fall limply at my sides as I replenish my oxygen supply.

Violet stays on top of me, her head on my shoulder, her breasts against my chest. She remains silent so I speak first.

"So, how was it?" I ask her.

"Good," she answers without lifting her head.

"Just good?"

She looks into my eyes. "Mind-blowing."

My lips curve into a smile. As I hold her gaze, I see the warmth clearly glistening in her blue eyes and my chest grows tight. That warmth, that softness—it makes me feel like coming home.

And I want to stay. I never want to leave.

I never want what we have to end.

I open my mouth to tell Violet that, but fear creates a lump in my throat.

What if this is just the sex talking? What if I change my mind later? What if Violet doesn't want a relationship with me? She may be having sex with me now, but I don't know if I've regained her trust. I don't know how she feels about me. I don't know what she wants.

Maybe it's too soon to tell her what I want.

"What is it?" Violet asks.

I realize my mouth is still open. I close it and clear my throat. Then I speak.

"Would you like to come to Toronto with me next weekend?"

CHAPTER EIGHTEEN

Violet

I've been to a lot of places but I've never been to Toronto, which is why I was thrilled when Asher asked me to visit the city with him. Some of my excitement vanished when I found out that the trip was work-related and not a romantic getaway Asher had thought of, but I was excited just the same.

Now that I'm here, I'm glad I came.

Asher and I have adjoining rooms at The Ritz-Carlton. From my window, I can see the trees shedding their fiery leaves in the park. I can see colorful benches and towering buildings. I can enjoy a view of the CN Tower framed against the clear blue sky. I can even catch a glimpse of Lake Ontario.

The lake. Somehow I always find myself in cities on lakes. And I always make good memories in them. Maybe the same will happen here.

I glance at the dress that I've laid out on my bed—a glittering purple dress that I bought back in Chicago with a pair of spaghetti straps, a sweetheart neckline and a slit on the right side that goes up past my knee. I've also brought a pair of gold sandals to go with it, dangling diamond earrings and a silver clutch purse.

Yup. I've come prepared. After all, tonight, I'm going to a party.

~

And boy, what a party it is.

It's at the Royal Ontario Museum, a magnificent building with walls that seem to be whispering stories, the legendary kind, not the scary kind. For tonight, specific items from every exhibit have been brought out into the lobby, each one fascinating. But I suppose the guests are the main exhibit—the women in their dazzling gowns, the men in their impeccable suits.

Speaking of suits, I think the award for the best one should go to the man standing right next to me. His is a sleek, bespoke, navy blue Tom Ford ensemble and it just screams sexy, powerful. No wonder the women are staring. They're looking at me, too, but mostly with glares or questioning glances, like they're wondering who I am and what

I did to deserve this man, which they probably think I don't. I don't care.

I'm the one Asher brought to this party.

As we go about socializing with other corporate executives and even some politicians and celebrities, I'm reminded of the party at Lloyd Finley's, the first one we went to together years ago. There are similarities. Top-notch crowd. High fashion. Small pieces of food. Champagne. Violins. The difference? This time, I'm not a graduate student looking at future job prospects, trying to impress. This time, I'm a corporate executive myself, representing a prestigious company, which means I'm just here to have fun.

The thought of that makes me smile, but another makes me frown.

I have the same date I did five years ago. And he hurt me five years ago. He abandoned me. He broke my heart. What if he does the same now?

I glance at Asher. Maybe he won't because we're sleeping together now. But that doesn't necessarily mean he's changed. He may have told me we're having more than just sex, but he hasn't asked to be my boyfriend. Will he ever? Can I trust him not to abandon me again? He said he isn't having sex with any other woman at the moment. Can I believe that? Can I trust him not to cheat on me?

"What's wrong?" Asher asks me after sipping his champagne.

I shake my head. "Nothing."

What am I doing worrying about things while I'm at a party?

Asher puts his glass down. "Would you like to dance?"

I grin. "I thought you'd never ask."

He leads me to the dance floor and we dance. Not like before, of course. We can't be that... uncivilized. He grips my waist and I grip his shoulders and we sway to the music like a couple at a prom or at a wedding.

Like a couple.

I look at Asher's face.

It would be nice if we could be a couple.

Asher's eyes narrow. "What is it?"

"Nothing," I tell him the same thing I said earlier.

His expression tells me he doesn't believe me.

"Violet..."

"Asher?" A voice interrupts us. "Asher Hawthorne?"

We stop dancing and turn our heads to see a man walking towards us. A familiar-looking man.

"Lloyd Finley?" I ask.

He grins. "Yes, it's me."

Who would have thought?

"I'm sorry. You are?"

"Vi—"

"Wait." He cuts me off and scratches his chin. "You were the one who came with him to that party at my house, right? I remember you were looking everywhere for Asher."

I nod. "Right."

He turns to Asher and nudges his arm. "You really shouldn't worry a woman like that, man. She thought you'd been killed or something."

Except he'd just run off with another woman.

Asher doesn't reply to Lloyd's remark. He pats him on the shoulder.

"Lloyd Finley. To think I'd see you here."

He shrugs. "What can I say? I love parties."

"That you do," Asher and I agree at the same time.

I chuckle at our synchronization.

Lloyd grins. "Well, I'm glad to see that the two of you are still together."

He thinks we are?

"Oh no." I wave my hand. "Asher and I aren't... I mean we didn't..."

"We're just friends," Asher says. "And colleagues. She works for the family company now."

Lloyd nods. "I see. That's good to know."

Not for me. I'm just a friend to Asher? Just a colleague? I know we're not boyfriend and girlfriend, but couldn't he have just said we're dating? He didn't even say anything when Lloyd was talking about that night. He could have apologized for all the trouble or say he'd never make me worry again. But it seems like he just wants to pretend it never happened.

Come to think of it, he's been like this from the beginning. He didn't want to talk about what happened at that party. He just wanted me to forgive him for it. And he doesn't want to talk about the fact that he sleeps around, either. When I asked him why, he just said it was because of the sex. So he slept with all those women just for sex. Now he's with me mostly for the sex, too. So how am I different?

What on earth am I doing?

"Excuse me," I speak up. "I have to go to the restroom."

I leave without waiting for either man to reply. Inside a cubicle, I lean against a wall and take deep breaths. I place my hand on my forehead as I think.

What am I doing here? Why am I with Asher when he tossed me aside like trash in the past? Why am I making the same mistake I made before, the one I swore I'd never make again?

I shake my head. No. I won't make the same mistake. Before things go any further, I'm going to talk to Asher. I'm going to find out for sure what his intentions are. I'm going to tell him that if he hurts me again, I'm not just going to knee him in the balls. I'm going to chop his dick off.

I get out of the restroom and head back to the dance floor. To my dismay, I don't see Asher. I only see Lloyd.

I approach him. "Have you seen Asher?"

He gives me a puzzled look. "Um, no. I thought he went after you."

"Oh. Okay."

As I head back to the restrooms, I can feel Lloyd's gaze following me. I know what he's thinking. That this is déjà vu. It kind of feels like it.

I check the area around the restrooms, figuring that maybe Asher did come after me but didn't see me come out. I don't see him. I start to look everywhere.

Yup. This is feeling like déjà vu.

Where are you, Asher?

Like before, I start to feel afraid as the time passes, thinking something bad might have happened to him. And I hate it. I hate that I still care so much. I hate thinking that if something bad happened to him, I'd be devastated. And I don't even have a right to be since we're not a couple.

Fuck.

Finally, I find him. In an empty corridor. With a woman in a blue gown.

I don't even have a chance to feel relief at finding him. My heart just shatters. I can't breathe.

I can't believe I'm going through this nightmare all over again.

As tears sting the back of my eyes, I pick up my skirt and run in the opposite direction.

"Violet!"

CHAPTER NINETEEN

Asher

I call after Violet but she doesn't stop running. I run after her down the other corridor, past the rope barrier and the sign that says the area is closed.

"Violet!"

She goes into a room and closes the door. Not just closes. Locks. I draw a deep breath.

"Violet, open the door," I tell her calmly.

"Go away," she says from the other side.

"I won't. And if you don't open this door, I'm going to do one of two things. One, I'm going to start banging my fists on this door, which will surely get the attention of the other guests and the reporters at the party, not to mention security. Or two, I'm just going to break this door down, which I suppose will cause an even bigger ruckus and possibly land me in jail."

Violet still doesn't open the door.

"Violet."

Finally, she does but just a crack.

"Why can't you just leave me alone?"

The distraught look on her face and the agony in her voice makes me frown. I definitely can't leave her alone now.

I step inside the room, which I realize is full of ancient tapestries, and close the door behind me.

"I'm not going anywhere, Violet," I tell her. "I came to this party with you and I'm not leaving without you."

"Why not? Because it might look bad? Who cares? You didn't care about that before. You didn't care that I was scared and I looked like a fool, which by the way, is what happened again." She slaps her forehead. "God, I can't believe I let this happen again."

"It's not happening again. I didn't leave you. I was just talking to someone—Patricia Heather. She works at the New York Stock Exchange and she knows my father."

Violet glares at me. "Do you think I care who she is?"

I frown. "I was just talking to her, alright? I've never slept with her and I wasn't planning to."

"Yeah, right."

She turns her back on me. I exhale.

"What? Are you going to bite my head off every time I talk to another woman? Am I not allowed to do that now?"

Violet turns around and points a finger at me. "Don't you dare make me sound like I'm a crazy, jealous, insecure girlfriend, because I'm not! You know why? Because I'm not even your girlfriend! I'm just your friend, remember? And your 'colleague'. Isn't that what you told Lloyd Finley?"

"Oh, is that what this is about now? Me not telling Lloyd Finley that we're not having sex? Well, excuse me, but I don't broadcast my sex life."

"That is not what I wanted you to say."

"Then what did you want me to say?" I ask her.

Instead of answering, she grips her hair in frustration and walks to the far side of the room. Then to my surprise, she crouches on the floor and starts sobbing.

Fuck.

What do I do? Do I just walk away and leave her alone like she asked? Do I drag her out of here?

Then I hear Stella's voice in my head.

Try harder. Do better.

I just have to get through to her.

I walk over to her. "Violet."

When she doesn't answer, I grab her arm. She pushes my hand away.

"Don't touch me."

At the sight of the tears trickling down her cheeks, a lump forms in my throat. I've seen Violet on the verge of tears before, but I've never actually seen her crying. Now that I do, my chest feels painfully tight.

Is this how she looked the night I left her at Lloyd Finley's party?

I hurt her then. And I just hurt her again. I feel guilty, foolish. I feel like the worst man in the world.

I dry her cheeks and stroke them as I look into her eyes.

"I'm sorry, Violet. I'm sorry I left you at Lloyd Finley's party. I'm sorry for making you worry just now."

Violet says nothing but her sobs seem to lessen.

I cup her face and kiss her cheeks.

"I'm sorry that I used to be a man-whore."

"Used to be?" she asks me as she wipes the corner of her eye.

I stroke her hair. "Now I'm just a man who can't get enough of you."

Violet's blue eyes grow wide. A blush coats her cheeks.

She's stopped crying. Good. But that doesn't mean I no longer want to kiss her or hold her in my arms.

I press my lips tenderly to hers. When she responds, my heart leaps against the walls of my chest. Heat flows through my veins.

I really can't get enough of her.

I slip my hand beneath Violet's hair to caress the nape of her neck as I push my tongue past her lips. To my surprise, she opens her mouth and captures the tip, sucking on it. I grin.

It seems like Violet can't get enough of me, either.

I run my hands across the bare skin of her upper back. She unbuttons my jacket and slips her hands beneath it to grip my waist. Then she pulls away and looks at me with furrowed eyebrows.

"Should we do this here?"

She's worried about that now?

"Do you really want to stop?" I ask her as I kiss her neck. "Because to be honest, I don't think I can."

"But…"

I take her hand and press her palm against the bulge in my crotch.

"Oh," she says.

"Don't worry." I kiss the other side of her neck. "We donated a lot of money, so this should be fine."

"But you said earlier that—"

I cut her off with a kiss. She kisses me back and rubs her palm against my clothed erection. It swells and I pull away to suck in a breath.

"I thought you wanted to stop," I say in a strained voice.

Violet gives my cock a squeeze. "Just shut up and fuck me."

I chuckle. "Yes, ma'am."

She frowns. "Did you just call me—?"

I kiss her again so she can't say another word. Then I carry her in my arms to the cushioned bench. I set her down and plant kisses on her neck and shoulders as I slip my hands beneath her gown. My fingers find the garter of her panties and I slowly pull it down her legs all the way past her knees to her ankles and off her sandals. I roll the panties into a ball and shove them inside the empty back pocket of my trousers. Then I start to free my belt from its buckle.

Violet interrupts me as she pushes off my jacket. I get rid of it and throw it on the bench. Then I continue with my efforts to free my cock. I get my belt free and unbutton my trousers. I unzip it and take my cock out of my boxers. Violet grabs my tie and pulls me forward to kiss me as she strokes it.

Naughty.

I return her kisses and let her play with me as my way of atoning for making her worry earlier. I'd let her play as much as she likes, but we don't exactly have the luxury of time.

The possibility that you might get caught is what makes sex in public exciting, but all the fun goes away if that ever turns into reality. I'd rather not get caught. I'm sure Violet would prefer that, too.

After about a minute, I push her hand away. I put a condom on and have her lie down on the bench. I roll her gown up to her waist.

"Hold it," I tell her to make sure the gown doesn't get in the way.

Violet clutches the fabric. I put one of my knees on the bench so that I'm straddling one of her legs, my other leg still against the floor. Then I issue another order.

"Turn the upper part of your body sideways."

When she does, I grab her other leg and lift it. I wrap my arm around her lower leg to hold it in place as I push the tip of my cock inside her. She gasps. I draw a deep breath and slowly push the rest of my cock in.

Once it's halfway in, I stop. I brush Violet's hair aside so I can see her face. Her eyes are closed. Her lips are pursed to hold back her moans. I stroke her cheek and she turns her head to look at me. Desire coats her eyes in place of tears, which frankly suits her better. Her lips part.

"Violet." Her name leaves my lips in a whisper as I hold her gaze.

I run my thumb over her lips in a tender caress because I can't kiss her in this position. Then I grip the back of the bench and start to move.

The bench creaks. Again, Violet closes her eyes and purses her lips. Her fingers tremble as they clutch her gown and gather it up to her chest.

I reach for one of her breasts as I continue with my thrusts. Her stiff nipple pokes my palm. In doing so, my angle must have shifted, because the muffled sounds she's making change. They're more intense now. She can barely keep them at bay.

I continue pounding into her from this new angle while keeping her breast in my hand. After a few more thrusts, she lifts her gown to her mouth to stifle her cries as she trembles. The passage around my cock tightens.

Fuck.

I let go of her breast to grip the back of the bench and put more power into my thrusts. I clench my jaw as I manage a few more. Then I give one final thrust.

I bury myself to the hilt inside Violet's still trembling body. She lets out a loud gasp followed by an unrestrained cry. I grunt as the heat from my balls spills out of my cock into its rubber sheath.

Afterwards, we both fall silent. I take just a moment to catch my breath before pulling out and getting rid of the used condom in a trash can in the corner.

As I fix my trousers, Violet gets off the bench. She stands up and her gown rolls back into place, down to her ankles without a crease as if nothing happened. I can't even tell she's not wearing any panties. But she can.

"Where are my panties?" she asks.

I reluctantly take them out of my pocket and throw them at her. As she puts them on, I grab my coat and put it back on. She buttons it and straightens my tie. I try to fix her hair as best as I can.

"How do I look?" Violet asks.

"Great," I answer.

It's not a lie. Some strands of her hair may be out of place now, but she still looks hot. In fact, I daresay she looks even hotter.

She sighs. "I can't believe we just had sex in a museum."

"They'd probably be happy to have us as part of their exhibit. People could learn a lot of things from us, you know."

Violet hits my shoulder playfully. "Shut up."

I smile. Just as I hoped, she seems to be in a better mood. Then again, who wouldn't be after the sex we just had?

"I still prefer having sex where there's no danger of being caught," she says. "Or interrupted."

I take her hand. "Then it's a good thing we have hotel rooms waiting."

Violet grins. "It sure is."

CHAPTER TWENTY

Violet

I sure am such a fool.

Yes, Toronto was fun. After the party, Asher and I went back to the hotel and had sex pretty much all night. Then we had lunch at the CN Tower, climbed to the SkyPod to take in the views, and took the flight home in the company's private jet. It was a short trip but memorable just the same.

But I'm not in Toronto anymore.

Now that I'm back in my apartment in Chicago, soaking in the tub as per my Sunday evening ritual and relaxing my tired muscles, my worries return. My mind is supposed to be taking a break before another workweek starts. Instead, my thoughts are bouncing around like the metallic ball in a pinball machine.

So what is going on with Asher and me again?

All he said was that he can't get enough of me, that and that he's sorry for being a man-whore. But he didn't say anything about starting a relationship and doing his best to make it work. He didn't say anything about loving me or wanting to stay by my side.

All he said was that he can't get enough of me. Of all of me? Or just sex with me? Because that much is obvious. But what happens when he gets tired of me? When he gets bored? Everyone gets enough of something at some point. The only reason they keep going is because they decide they want more.

That's the thing. It has to be a decision. Asher has to decide that he wants to be with me. This thing between us can't just be a thing that happens. Or it can unhappen with the snap of a finger.

I know it's what Asher is used to. He goes to a bar or a club and a woman flirts with him. Or maybe he sees a woman and flirts. Either way, it just happens and then they just end up having sex. And then it's over. But it's not like he planned on everything being that way. If he didn't find a woman, that was fine, though I have a feeling that doesn't happen much. If he didn't like the woman, he wasn't going to have sex with her. If the woman didn't want to have sex with him, he wasn't going to force it. They just happened to meet. They have no obligation to do anything with each other. They just do because they want to have fun.

Isn't what Asher and I have pretty much the same except maybe an extended version?

I can't have that. Maybe Asher can, but I can't. We can't have just a thing. We have to call it something. We have to decide to call it something. We're not sixteen or nineteen where we can do something and just wait and see where it goes. I can't. I'm twenty-nine. I don't want to waste time. If Asher has no intention of making this, whatever it is, go somewhere, I want to know. If he does, I want to know that, too.

I want to know his intentions. I'm too old to play guessing games and I have a right to know.

I have to know.

~

"Then you just have to ask," Michelle tells me during lunchtime the next day. "It's that simple."

Everything is simple to her. Maybe that's how it seems when you're on the outside looking in, when you're not actually tangled in the mess.

I stick my fork into the cherry tomato on my plate and pop it inside my mouth. "I've already asked. Twice, I think."

Didn't I ask him at the museum? Or did I?

"Then ask again," Michelle says. "And this time, make sure you get a clear answer. Ask him a yes or no question. Then he'll have nowhere to hide."

I look at her. "Why didn't I think of that?"

She shrugs. "Maybe because you don't really want to know the answer?"

I snort. That's absurd.

"Are you ready to hear his answer, Violet?" Michelle asks me. "If he says no, are you ready to have your heart broken again? Can you handle it?"

I don't think anyone is ready to have their heart broken. It's something no one would ask for. But I can handle it if that's what has to happen. I've survived before.

"And if he says yes, are you ready to start a relationship with him knowing that it failed the last time?"

That's a tougher question. Am I ready? Am I willing to really give Asher a chance and make this work?

"I'll think about it," I answer. "I'll make my decision. But first, I have to know his."

"So if he says no, you'll just let him go and if he says yes, you'll maybe have a relationship with him?"

I shrug. "I'll think about it, but I can't be the only one."

Michelle nods. "Right. If you're going to make this work, both of you have to decide that you're going to make it work."

"Exactly. There has to be a mutual decision, an agreement."

"A commitment."

Precisely. That's exactly what I'm looking for, but I'm afraid it might not be in Asher's vocabulary. It seems like he's never committed himself to anyone, and I don't know if he's capable of it. I tried to discern it when I asked him why he sleeps around, but I didn't really get much of an answer. He didn't want to talk about it, which likely means he has commitment issues.

Can he commit himself to me?

Michelle places her hand over mine. "So, when are you going to ask him?"

~

I draw a deep breath as I stand in front of the door to Asher's office. I can feel Dylan's gaze on me, waiting for me to knock, wondering why I'm nervous. Frankly, I don't know why I am either. I ignore him and knock on the door. It takes a few seconds before I hear Asher's voice.

"Come in."

I step inside. As my gaze meets Asher's, he smiles.

"Violet."

That's a good thing, right? Him calling me by my first name. But I don't want to rely on signs anymore.

I return his smile. "Asher."

He leaves his desk and walks towards me. Before I can say another word, his lips are on mine. Smooth. Warm. Making mine tingle.

Damn it. Why is he so good at kissing?

He pulls away and touches my cheek. His eyes gaze into mine.

"I haven't seen you since yesterday."

It takes me a moment to answer because my mind seems to be reeling.

"I know."

We were supposed to have dinner together but he got busy. I, too, remembered I had stuff to get ready for work, which I dove into right away after I arrived this morning.

Asher strokes my cheek. "I've missed you."

I almost say the words back but something clicks inside my head. I remember what I came here for.

I clear my throat. "Asher, I'm not just here to check on you."

He leans forward and brings his mouth close to my ear. "Naughty."

In spite of myself, I blush.

He starts to lick my ear. I place my hand on his chest and push him away.

"I'm not here for that, either," I tell him. "Asher, we need to talk."

"About?" He grabs my hand and rubs my palm.

It's distracting so I pull my hand away.

"Us."

"What about us?"

"Exactly," I say. "What about us? What are we?"

Asher frowns. "I thought we already talked about this."

"We tried to, but I didn't really get a straight answer. So I'm going to ask you again." I draw another deep breath. "Is this... going somewhere?"

It's not what I was supposed to ask, but my script seems to have evaporated from my head.

Asher grabs my hand, pulls me close and puts his hand back on my cheek.

"Haven't we already been places?"

I frown. He's not taking me seriously at all.

He goes behind me and puts his hands on my shoulders.

"Speaking of going somewhere, I was thinking we should go on another trip. Just the two of us again, but this time, with nothing related to work to worry about. What do you think?"

"That... sounds good," I admit.

"Really?"

Wait a second. Why am I answering his question when he hasn't answered mine?

I turn around to face him. "Asher..."

"What about we go to Finland? We can stay in a glass igloo and watch the Northern Lights. Or we can go to Japan. They have nice trains and hot springs…”

“Asher.” I grip his arms. “Before I go anywhere with you, tell me. Are you serious about me?”

There. I've gone and said it.

But Asher just grins. “I seriously want you right now.”

Seriously?

“Asher, I…”

He seals my lips with his own before I can say more. Firmly. Passionately.

I try to resist but I don't have the strength, and when his tongue brushes against mine, even my will starts to melt. The thoughts inside my head spin. My knees tremble.

Somehow, my hands end up on Asher's hips. He caresses the nape of my neck, then my back. His fingers run along the zipper of my dress.

When he starts to pull it down, something in me snaps.

No. This is not what we're supposed to be doing. This is not what we're doing.

I try to pull away but he wraps his arm around me. His hand clenches my ass.

"Asher," I tell him as I manage to break the kiss.

He plants his mouth on my neck instead.

"I'm serious, Violet," he says. "I want you right now."

"But I don't," I tell him. "I want to talk."

He kisses my ear. "We can talk later."

"No. We'll talk right now. You will answer my question right now."

He kisses my shoulder. "I thought I already did."

"No, you didn't."

"Then this is my answer." He presses his lips to the top of my breast. "After all, actions speak louder than words, right?"

"Not now." I push him away. "Now, I need you to tell me your answer. Out loud. And clear."

His lips return to my neck. His hand runs down my side.

"Isn't this clear enough for you?"

My patience reaches its limit. Okay. Enough. No more fun and games. No more of this foolishness.

If he says this is his answer, then I guess the message is clear. He's not serious about me at all. He only wants sex. He doesn't care about how I feel or what I have to say.

In that case, there's no point continuing this any longer.

"Asher, let me go!"

I try to push him away again but he doesn't budge. I beat my fists on his chest.

"Asher, stop! I—"

Just then, the door opens. Asher stops. I freeze, too, as I see who's standing in the doorway.

Ryker Hawthorne and his older brother, Ethan, who now has a look of disappointment on his face.

"What the hell is going on here?"

CHAPTER TWENTY-ONE

Asher

I take my hands off Violet and face my brothers. What the hell? What the fuck are they doing in my office?

"Ms. Cleary," Ethan addresses Violet. "Did Asher do anything to you?"

"No," she answers, and then she rushes out of the room.

I get an urge to go after her, but I don't. Something tells me she's not going to listen to me anyway. Besides, I can't just run away from my brothers.

Ryker sighs. "Her actions sure tell a different story."

I ignore him and go behind my desk. "What are the two of you doing here?"

"We just wanted to know how the fundraiser went," Ethan says. "Believe it or not, we didn't come here just to bust your ass, but it seems to be a good thing we did."

I snort.

Ethan places his hands on my desk. "What were you doing to Violet?"

"The fundraiser went well," I inform him. "I donated exactly how much you said I should and mingled with some people we do business with. Now, can you get out of my office?"

Ethan shakes his head. "You still haven't grown up, have you, Asher?"

I glare at him. "I said get out of my office."

"You don't scare me," he says. "And you don't have the right to send me away. We both know that. But just in case you forgot, tell him why, Ryker."

"Because he's your boss," Ryker says.

I shrug. "So what? He can have sex in his office and I can't?"

Ethan draws a breath.

"Or is the problem that Violet is my subordinate?" I ask him. "Oh, but wait. Wasn't Stella your assistant when you started fu—"

"Don't you dare bring Stella into this," he cuts me off. "Neither of those are the problems. The problem is that Violet didn't look like she was willing. It looked like you were forcing yourself on her."

"I wasn't," I tell him.

I felt her resisting me. I knew she wanted to stop. And I was about to. I just didn't do it right away because there was a voice in my head telling me that if I did, she'd slip through my fingers, which is exactly what happened.

Fuck.

I shake my head. "You don't know anything about us."

"Then tell me something." Ethan crosses his arms over his chest. "Are you and Violet Cleary in a relationship?"

Weird. Isn't that what Violet was asking me?

"We're sleeping together if that's what you're asking," I answer. "Not that it's any of your business."

Ethan sighs.

"And we did go on a date at the Navy Pier."

"You did?" Ryker asks. "Isn't that a first?"

"So you're serious about her?" Ethan asks.

Again, same question. I'm sick of it.

I stand up and bunch my shoulders. "Why does everyone have to be so serious? And why is everyone poking their nose into my fucking business?”

I point to the door to my office.

“Get out.”

Neither Ethan nor Ryker moves.

“I said get out!”

“Fine,” Ethan says finally. “Let’s go, Ryker. He’s old enough to sort out his own messes.”

“Yes, I am,” I tell him. “Thank you.”

They walk out the door. I sink back into my chair and let out a breath of relief.

“And thank you for leaving.”

I grab the glass of water on my desk and take a long sip.

Now, finally, I can have some peace and quiet in my office. Or so I think until I remember Violet and how she marched off.

Why was she so pissed? I already told her I can’t get enough of her, which is not something I’ve told any woman before. I told her I’m not having sex with anyone else. Again, not something I usually say. And I even said just a while ago that I missed her. Hasn’t she been listening? Isn’t it enough? Why won’t she believe me? What more does she want from me? Does she want me to propose to her? Is that it?

I shake my head. Women. Why can't they ever be satisfied? Why do they always have something to complain about? Why can't they be reasonable?

I put my glass down and let out a deep breath.

Oh well. I guess I'll just have to talk to her later.

~

I tuck my hands into my pockets and tap my foot on the floor as I wait for Violet to open the door to her apartment.

I've already rung the doorbell three times. I know she's in there because I can see the light coming from under the door and I can hear the TV. Yet for some reason, she's not coming.

Is she in the bathroom? Does she have earphones on? Or is she just pretending she can't hear me?

Come on, Violet.

I ring the doorbell again. When she still doesn't answer, I start knocking.

"Violet?"

Still nothing.

A new idea forms in my mind. What if she's not coming to the door because she can't? What if she's hurt? What if she needs help?

My chest tightens. I bang my fists on the door.

"Violet, are you in there? Answer the door!"

No answer.

"Violet!"

Finally, I hear footsteps coming. The door opens and Violet appears in a shirt and pajama pants. I place my hand over my chest as I let out a breath of relief.

"Thank God. For a moment there, I was worried something bad had happened to you."

"You mean like how I felt when I couldn't find you at Lloyd Finley's party?" she tells me. "Or at the museum? Good."

She's mad. Really mad.

I draw a deep breath. "Can we talk?"

Her eyebrows arch. "Oh, now you want to talk? Well, I don't."

Violet tries to close the door in my face. I use my shoulder and my foot to keep it open.

"Really?" Violet gives me a look of resentment as she drops her shoulders. "You really don't know how to take no for an answer, do you?"

"I'm not going away until we talk," I tell her. "Or would you rather have this conversation at work?"

She puts her hands on her hips. "So, what did your brothers think about that, huh? I bet you got scolded."

"I don't care about them. I care about you. That's why I'm here."

"Oh, really? You care about me?" She points her fingers at her chest, then waves her hands. "Don't worry. I can handle your brothers."

"I said they're not why I'm here."

"Why are you here, then, Asher?" Her hands go back to her hips. "Because you weren't able to have your fun earlier? Because you can't get enough of fucking me?"

I frown. "That's not what I said."

"What exactly can't you get enough of, then?" She crosses her arms beneath her breasts. "Go on. Tell me."

"You," I tell her. "All of you."

Her eyebrows go up. "All of me? Really?"

I pinch the bridge of my nose as I try to get a hold of my temper. Why is Violet being so difficult?

I inhale then exhale. "Violet…"

"Why don't you just admit it, Asher? That all you want from me is sex?"

My temper slips. I shake my head.

"You know what? If you don't want to believe me, there's nothing I can do. If you want to make fun of me, fine. But I'm not going to put up with any of this."

I step back.

Violet snorts. "Oh, now you're leaving?"

I meet her gaze. "I thought you wanted me to leave."

"I thought you wanted to talk."

"I did, but you're clearly not in the mood. All you want to do is pick a fight."

"Really?" Violet steps forward. "So I'm the bad guy here, am I? I'm the crazy bitch?"

I shrug. "You did stick your knee into my balls."

She shakes her head. "Unbelievable."

For once, we agree. This whole conversation, if it can even be called one, is ridiculous.

I walk away.

"That's right, Asher Hawthorne," Violet tells me. "Leave. That's what you're good at, right? You leave your date at a party so she doesn't have a ride home."

I stop in my tracks and roll my eyes. I guess she'll never forgive me for that.

"And then you leave the women you sleep with behind on the bed right after you get your pants back on. And you never look back. You just throw them away and forget they ever existed."

I turn around. "But I didn't do that to you, did I?"

Violet doesn't answer.

"You know I didn't, but it doesn't mean anything to you."

"I don't know what it means," she says. "Tell me what it means, Asher. That's all I'm asking."

"No. That's not all you're asking. You want me to give you a ring."

"I never said that."

"You want me to say I'm in love with you and I can't live without you. Isn't that right?"

Violet purses her lips and says nothing. She doesn't have to. I know I'm right. I also know I can't say those words. Not yet.

I shake my head. "Even if I say those words, you're not going to believe me anyway, are you?"

Violet meets my gaze. There isn't any trace of anger in her eyes now. Just pain.

A lump forms in my throat. What? Is she going to cry again? But I have a feeling that this time, she isn't going to let me comfort her.

"That's the thing with faith, Asher," she says in a breaking voice. "It has to be earned. And no, you haven't earned it."

So that's what this all comes to? That's her decision? That she doesn't want to have anything to do with me anymore? Then I guess I have no choice but to respect it.

I nod. "Fine. Just remember that I'm not the one who threw what we had away."

I turn away, but instead of going to my apartment, I walk past Violet to the elevator. I'm not staying here tonight, maybe not for a while. She can cry all she wants. She can break all the stuff in her apartment, but I don't want to hear any of it. I don't want to know.

If she wants nothing to do with me, then this time, for once, I'm going to leave her alone.

CHAPTER TWENTY-TWO

Violet

I close the door behind me and lean on it.

For a moment, I just stay there. I don't have the strength to move. My mind, which has been filled with all sorts of chaotic notions, suddenly feels empty. My body feels numb. My heart feels like it's no longer in my chest, like it's been shattered into a million pieces and those fragments have started to evaporate one by one.

Weird. It almost feels like I usually do after an orgasm—adrift like I'm out of my body, hollow, undone. Who knew pain could have the same effect?

I am in pain. I don't know exactly what part of me is aching. I don't even know if it's my body that hurts. I don't know why I'm hurting. I just know I am.

The strength leaves my legs and I slide down towards the floor. My legs spread out before me. My arms lie limp at my sides. A tear trickles down my cheek.

Why does it hurt so much?

It didn't hurt nearly this much five years ago. I cried, too, yes. I felt sick to my stomach, too. When I got back to my apartment, I just lay in my bed in my dress for a while. But it didn't hurt this much. This time, I can barely breathe. This time, I feel like something more has been taken from me. Something real and important.

But of course it would hurt more. After all, five years ago, I barely knew Asher. I cried mostly because I felt like trash, because I felt stupid. I blamed myself for my suffering. But now, I'm crying because Asher and I had something and now it's gone. He said I threw it away, and a part of me believes that. But it's not entirely my fault. I wanted to believe in Asher, but how could I when he wouldn't give me a reason to believe? I wanted to be with him, but he didn't seem to feel that way. It even felt like he was refusing to feel that way.

He said I was asking for too much, but I felt like he wasn't giving me enough to hold on to. Was it really too much to ask for him to say he didn't believe in love but he was going to try anyway? I wasn't expecting him to say he loved me. After all, we still don't know each other that well. I wanted him to tell me how he felt. I wanted him to let me in. It's not so much that I wanted a label for whatever was going on between us, more like I wanted to know that we were in it together, no matter what it was.

I just wanted to know that Asher wasn't going to disappear like last time, or at least that he would try not to. Is that really too much to ask?

It's funny, isn't it? When you don't tell a man what you want, he thinks you're a coward, that you're a cocktease, that you're playing tricks on him. You tell him what you want and it becomes too much and he runs away like a scared little boy.

At any rate, it doesn't matter. Asher is gone. I've lost him. This time, I've really lost him. Before, I couldn't say that because I didn't really have him. He wasn't really mine. But now, I can say he was mine, even for just a short while. I had him. We had something. And now, it's gone. And it hurts so fucking much.

I clutch the front of my shirt as even more tears fall, silently, like raindrops making their way down a car window.

Why? Why did Asher and I have to meet again just for us to end up this way? Why did we have to be together again if we don't belong together, if he can't be with me anyway?

Asher has toyed with any number of women. Maybe I've played with a few hearts myself without knowing. But fate, fate is the real player. And the cruelest.

I hug my knees to my chest as I let out loud sobs, the pain too much for me to stay quiet.

Of course, I'm partly to blame, too. I'm angry at myself, too. I gave Asher a chance even though I said I wouldn't. I expected more from him even though I said we would just have meaningless sex. I knew he was a man-whore. I had a feeling he was incapable of commitment. Still, I hoped.

What's that saying? Fool me once, shame on you. Fool me twice, shame on me.

Shame. That's something I'll have to live with. Because I have to live. I have to keep going.

I'm hurting. I'm scarred. But I have to keep going.

I have to breathe. I have to get up. I have to eat, to sleep. I have to go to work tomorrow and the day after and the one after that even if I don't feel like it, even if I don't want to.

Because I have to live.

Right now, I'm dying, but I will live. I don't know how, but somehow, after these tears stop falling, I'll find a way to make it through.

But first, I have to breathe.

~

Breathe, Violet.

I tell myself that as I step out of the elevator and walk to my office, my shoulders pulled back and my chin high.

I have to pretend that this is just like any other day at the office. After all, for everyone else, it is. No one knows what happened between me and Asher. No one can see my broken heart even though I feel like it's hanging outside my chest. And no one has to know.

I've dried my tears. I've put on my makeup, including a generous amount of concealer. I have a nice dress. I have my full armor. I can't let anyone see through me.

As I pass by a row of cubicles, I feel some stares, and for a moment I get worried that they might have found out that Asher and I had a fight. But then I remember that yesterday, I fled Asher's office shortly after Ethan and Ryker showed up. That's probably why they're staring. That's probably what they're speculating about.

They can speculate all they want. I don't care.

I manage to get to my office just fine. Yes, I'm fine. I sit behind my desk and start to work. I'm off to a good start, too. But then, the worst happens.

Asher passes by. He passes in front of my office and turns his head so our eyes meet for just a moment, too brief to convey any meaning. Then he's gone. I freeze.

Once, when I was in an emergency room in Zurich because of a sprained ankle and I was waiting for the swelling to go down, I overheard the nurses talking. They were talking about one of their fellow nurses who had refused to show up to work because her boyfriend had broken up with her. I thought it was silly. Why refuse to work just because of a broken heart? Why not work so you can forget about your problem? That's what I normally do.

But now, I understand why someone wouldn't want to come to work after a breakup. And it's even harder when the one you broke up with is your boss.

I close my eyes and draw a deep breath.

Breathe, Violet. Just breathe.

~

I can't breathe.

I thought things would gradually get easier, but it's been three days and the pain remains as sharp. Each time I see Asher, I feel like my chest is being opened and my heart is being broken to pieces all over again.

And I've just seen Asher. We were just in a meeting together which lasted more than an hour, and the whole time I was sitting next to him pretending to be okay, trying not to look at him. But I ended up looking at him anyway, and I still couldn't help but think about how hot he is and I still ended up feeling miserable knowing he's no longer mine.

So here I am hiding in an empty cubicle, trying to breathe.

If I don't, I just know I'll start crying, and I can't do that right now.

Just breathe.

"There you are, Ms. Cleary," Asher's voice interrupts my breathing.

Fuck.

"I was wondering where you'd gone after the meeting. I just had to give you this."

He hands me a flash drive. I try to look at it instead of him.

"It contains the report we discussed during the meeting. I'd be happy if you added the items you suggested."

I nod. "Sure."

"Thank you."

He leaves.

Wow. That's it? Not so much as 'What are you doing hiding here?' or 'Are you okay?' He really no longer cares about me at all?

He's been cold to me before, but this is different. This is indifference. It makes me think he never really cared about me at all.

I run toward the restroom because I can no longer breathe and I just know I'm about to cry, but I bump into Stella on the way.

"I'm sorry," I tell her sincerely. "I didn't hurt the baby, did I?"

She touches her belly and shakes her head. "No, no. The baby's fine."

"Good. I'm sorry. Really, I am. But I have to go."

I start to run off.

"Violet?" Stella calls after me.

I stop.

"Are you okay?"

Tears sting the back of my eyes. Why did she have to ask me that question? Why did she have to care? Now, I feel... not okay.

"Violet?" Stella stands in front of me.

I say nothing. I can't speak. If I open my mouth, I might start sobbing.

She should just leave me alone before I explode into a mess.

But she doesn't. Instead, she grabs my hand and pulls me down the corridor. I'm confused.

"Where are we going?" I ask her.

"To have ice cream," she answers. "It looks like you need a few scoops."

~

I didn't realize I did until I finished four, which must be a record for me.

As I place the spoon I've licked clean in the empty bowl, I feel better. I also feel a bit colder, but I do feel better. It's like how you feel when you've been jogging for miles and you feel like giving up and then you suddenly feel this cold breeze on your face. Or like that snowball someone throws in your face when you don't want to play because you're sulking.

I feel better.

"Thanks," I tell Stella.

"For the ice cream? Don't thank me. These days, I can't get enough ice cream even though it's getting cold. I'm just glad I found someone to eat a heap with."

A heap? Come to think of it, she did eat even more than me—five scoops, I think. Or was it six?

"The ice cream was good," I tell her. "But I'm more grateful for the company."

"You're welcome," Stella answers. "And actually, the company would be happy to be of more help."

I give her a puzzled look. What was that?

"I mean if there's something on your mind that you'd like to share with me, I'd be happy to listen," Stella explains. "If you want, we can even order more ice cream, or maybe you can have coffee while you talk if that'll help."

I shake my head. "No, thanks. About the additional ice cream and the coffee, I mean."

"And the fact that I'm willing to listen?" Stella asks.

I glance at my watch. "I'd love to, but I should get back to the office. I didn't tell anyone I was leaving, so…"

"It's fine. If Asher asks you where you went, you can just say you were with me. He shouldn't complain then. If he does, I'll kick his ass."

My eyebrows furrow. "You can do that?"

She shrugs. "Well, maybe I shouldn't, but Ethan won't mind if I do."

My eyes grow wide. "So you really are going out with Ethan Hawthorne."

Stella gives me a puzzled look. "You didn't know?"

I shake my head. "I had my suspicions, but I didn't know it for sure."

She chuckles.

I guess that means everyone knows.

She shows me her hand. "Actually, Ethan and I are engaged."

"Whoa," I exclaim as I see the diamond ring. "So you're...?"

"Getting married? Yes, but after the baby is born. I don't think I can handle a wedding right now."

I guess it would be stressful trying to handle a wedding and a pregnancy at the same time.

"Congratulations," I tell her.

She smiles. "Thanks." Then she draws a breath. "So, you see, I promise you won't get in trouble if you don't go back to the office. Also, I may be practically Asher's sister-in-law, but I can still be your friend."

My eyes grow wide. "How did you know...?"

"I just had a feeling," Stella says.

I think it's more than that.

"If I'm right, then I may be able to help you more than you know. After all, I know how difficult the Hawthorne brothers can be."

"Even Ethan?" I ask her curiously.

"Especially Ethan."

She goes on to tell me how she and Ethan met, after which I feel obliged to tell her about what happened between me and Asher. I didn't think I'd be able to talk about it, but Stella is surprisingly easy to talk to. Also, it feels good to get everything off my chest.

"That Asher," Stella grumbles when I'm done talking. "Now I really want to kick his ass."

My eyebrows arch. She's on my side?

"So you think I did the right thing?" I ask her. "In confronting him and telling him I wanted nothing more to do with him?"

"You did the right thing." She pats my hand. "But you know what? If there's something I've learned, it's that doing the right thing doesn't necessarily make you happy. In fact, it rarely does."

Her statement takes me by surprise.

"So I shouldn't have done it?"

"I don't think it matters what you should have or shouldn't have done. You've already done it. What matters now is what you want to do next."

I sigh. "What do you think I should do?"

"Hmm." Stella touches her chin. "Maybe talk to Asher and give him another chance?"

"What?"

"I've told you this before. Asher may be a jerk. He may be awfully clueless about how other people feel. But he's not a bad person. I think all this time, he's been searching for someone he can really be with, someone who can really understand him and be there for him, someone who can love him and teach him how to love."

"You're saying I should teach him to love me?"

"You love him, don't you?"

That question takes me even more by surprise. What?

"I can see it in your eyes," Stella says. "I heard it in your voice."

She did?

"But you don't have to admit it to me. It's fine. You're the one who needs to know it."

But I don't know if I do.

"Even if you're right, I don't want to force someone to love me."

"I didn't say force," Stella says. "I said teach. Asher feels something for you. I'm sure of it. You just have to give him time to develop it into something more. You have to teach him how to."

I shake my head. "Why do I have to do that?"

"Because maybe he doesn't know how to love," Stella answers. "And maybe because those who do don't know how to give up on love."

I say nothing, but I'm starting to understand what Stella is saying. What if she's right? What if I asked too much of Asher like he said? What if I was too impatient? What if I didn't really give him a chance?

~

I'm still thinking about those questions as I cross the lobby of The Mistral.

What do I do? Do I just forget the fight Asher and I had and all the hurtful things he said to me? Why do I always have to be the one to do something, to give in, to take a leap of faith? Why can't he? Then again, can I stand not doing anything? Can I just leave things as they are?

Either way, I lose. And I hate losing. Isn't there another way?

I'm almost to the elevator when I hear someone call my name.

"Violet!"

At the thought that it might be Asher, my heart leaps. But then it sinks as I turn my head and realize it's not. It's just Liam.

Wait. Liam? All the way from Switzerland?

"Violet!" He puts his arms around me. "How are you?"

"Good," I answer automatically before giving him a puzzled look. "Liam, what are you doing here?"

CHAPTER TWENTY-THREE

Asher

What am I doing here?

Yesterday, I caught Violet hiding in a cubicle on the verge of tears. After that, she disappeared. Today, she didn't come in to work. According to Dylan, she isn't feeling well but it's nothing serious. Is that true? Something tells me it's a lie.

If it is, shouldn't I go check on her and ask her what's wrong? What if she's thinking of quitting because of me? And if it isn't a lie, shouldn't I go check on her and bring her something to make her feel better? She's still one of my most valuable employees.

Why am I still here at the office?

It's not because I no longer care. From the moment I saw her in her office the day after we had the fight, I realized I still do. And these past few days when Violet and I haven't been able to talk—talk, not just discuss things about work—these past few days when I haven't even seen Violet smile, I realized just how much.

I miss her. I miss her smile and the laughter which she always seems to be trying to suppress. I even miss her glares and her pouts and the way that she rolls her eyes and turns her nose up at me. I miss her hair and how it smells. I miss the warm softness of her lips. I miss the heat of her skin. I miss every nook and cranny of her beautiful body. I miss her pancakes. I miss her competitiveness, her stubbornness, her charm, her confidence and the vulnerability she's only showed to me.

I miss her. I miss all of her.

But do I have a right to? Do I have a right to miss her after I hurt her so much? Do I have a right to still care about her when I'm still not sure I can give her what she wants? Do I have a right to want her back?

I think about that for a few seconds. Then I slam my hands on my desk as I get out of my chair.

Fuck it. I'm going to go see her.

~

Almost as soon as I ring the doorbell, I hear someone rushing to the door. My heart races. My fingers tighten around the bouquet of flowers I have in my hand.

Then the door opens and I see a man in the doorway, a tall man with blond curls and pale skin wearing the Canadian flag sweater that Violet and I bought at the gift shop of CN Tower. I frown.

He gives me a huge smile. "Hi."

Who the hell is this guy? Why does he sound like he has a French accent? Or is it German? Most importantly, what is he doing in Violet's apartment?

He looks at the bouquet I'm holding. "You must be Asher."

He knows who I am?

"Yeah." I offer him my hand. "Asher Hawthorne."

"Liam O'Connell."

O'Connell? So he's Irish? That still doesn't explain who he is and what he's doing in Violet's apartment.

"Are those for Violet?" he asks about the bouquet.

I nod. "Yeah. I heard she wasn't feeling well. I'd like to see her and give this to her in person."

The man doesn't budge. He shakes his head.

"I'm sorry, but that's not possible."

I wonder if it's possible to punch him instead. But no. I'm not going to let my temper get the better of me this time.

I square my shoulders instead and stick my chest out.

"Maybe you didn't hear me. I'm Asher Hawthorne. I'm her—"

"I know exactly who you are."

And the hostility that has suddenly taken over his expression tells me how much else he knows.

Who is he that Violet confided in him so much? Her brother? I don't think she has one. Besides, they don't look at all alike.

It's unfair. He knows who I am and I know nothing about him.

I let out a breath. "So Violet doesn't want to see me. Is that it?"

"She's not here," Liam says.

So she was lying when she said she wasn't feeling well.

"Where is she?" I ask.

Liam shrugs. "She went to buy some food. She just left a few minutes ago. I don't know when she'll be back."

In other words, he wants me to leave. Should I?

I look at the bouquet in my hand. If Violet isn't here, there's no reason for me to stay. But should I leave the bouquet with this loser? I don't want to.

I leave. I don't even bother to tell the guy to tell Violet I was here. I have a feeling he won't.

"Aren't you leaving the flowers?" he asks.

I lift them. "I'll just give them to her next time."

I proceed to the elevator thinking our conversation has ended, but the man speaks again.

"Wouldn't it be better if you just stayed away from her?" he asks. "Haven't you hurt her enough?"

I stop in my tracks. My hands clench into fists. If he wasn't making any sense, I would have punched him already, but as much as I hate to admit it, he may be right. Maybe it is better for me to stay away from Violet.

I look at the bouquet I'm holding. Then I turn around and throw it at him. It almost lands on his surprised face but ends up in his arms.

It's his now. Just like Violet.

She and I are done.

As I step inside the elevator, I try to convince myself that I just did the right thing, that it's for the best.

But then why does it feel like shit?

~

"You look like shit," Ethan says as he slides on top of the stool beside me. "How many martinis have you had?"

"Oh, he didn't have any martinis," Glenn answers for me. "He's been drinking gin straight up. And he's been here since three."

"Three in the afternoon?" I hear the surprise in Ethan's voice.

"Someone played hooky," Ryker mutters.

"Shut up, Ryker," I tell him as I lift my head off the counter.

I look at Glenn and raise a finger.

"Another glass of gin, please."

"No," Ethan says. "No more gin."

I glare at him. "You can't tell me what to do here. We're not at the office. You're not my boss."

He sips his whiskey and says nothing. Now what? He's ignoring me?

I turn to Ryker. "Ryker, tell Ethan he's not my boss here."

"I don't think you should have any more gin either," he says.

I frown. "Did I ask for your opinion?"

"You're drunk," Ethan tells me. "As soon as I'm done with my drink, I'm bringing you home."

"I'm not drunk," I reply.

I know I've been here for hours and drunk four glasses of gin, maybe more. I know that I feel a little lightheaded. And I can smell the alcohol on my breath. But I'm not drunk.

"You are drunk," Ryker seconds.

I look at him. "Again, I wasn't asking for your opinion."

He shrugs. "It doesn't make it any less true."

"And I'm not going home," I tell Ethan. "I'm not going back to my apartment."

"Why not?" he asks.

"Because Violet is there."

"I thought she lives there," Ryker says.

I ignore him. "And her new boyfriend."

Ethan puts his glass down. "I see. So you got yourself drunk because Violet dumped you and got a new boyfriend."

"I am not drunk."

"But you got dumped?" Ryker asks. "Well, isn't that a first?"

I glare at him. "Shut up, Ryker."

"I don't see how her new boyfriend is your problem," Ethan says. "After all, she already dumped you."

I fight the urge to cover my ears. Can they please stop saying 'dumped'?

"Maybe he's still in love with her," Ryker says. "Wait. Isn't that a first, too?"

I give him another glare. Does he want me to punch him? Because if he does, I'd be happy to oblige. My fist is still itching from this afternoon.

"So you finally fell in love with someone but then you let her slip through your fingers," Ethan says. "Don't worry. It happens to the best of men, especially those who've never been in love before."

"Are you speaking from experience?" I ask him.

He doesn't answer that. Instead, he looks at me.

"You know what you have to do? You have to get her back. That's what you and Ryker told me when I lost Stella. You told me to go after her and get her back. So you do the same. Get her back."

I snort and let my chin fall on the counter. "It's not that easy."

"Because she has a new boyfriend?"

"Because she wants me to be her boyfriend and I'm not sure I'm ready to be that," I confess. "And I don't know how to be."

"Did you tell her that?"

I pause. "No."

"I'm guessing you haven't told her you're in love with her, either," Ryker says.

"Because I'm not," I tell him.

"Oh yes you are," Ryker says.

This time, I don't protest. I just wonder. Am I?

"Just go and tell her how you feel," Ethan tells me. "Everything you feel. If she decides she still wants nothing to do with you, then let her go. Just don't give up before putting up a fight."

I chuckle. "Funny. Stella told me the same thing."

"You talked to her?" Ethan asks.

"When I went to your house after I found out Violet and I were neighbors," I tell him.

"Oh." Ethan nods. "Well, anyway, we're both right. You shouldn't be here drinking, not until you've really lost."

"Haven't I?"

"Have you given up?" Ryker asks me.

"I gave her new boyfriend flowers," I answer.

"What?" they both say at the same time.

"I gave her new boyfriend the flowers I was going to give her. That's like throwing in the towel, right?"

Ryker laughs. "You did what?"

"So you did something stupid," Ethan says. "So what? That doesn't mean you've given up on Violet, does it?"

"I don't think so," I answer.

Ethan grabs my shoulder and straightens me up. He looks into my eyes.

"Do you want Violet back, Asher Hawthorne?"

"Yes," I answer without thinking.

"Then go get her back," Ethan tells me.

"Okay."

"Though maybe not right now," Ryker says. "She won't take you seriously if you're drunk. Plus you might throw up on her in front of her new boyfriend, which won't help you win her back at all."

"Fine." I agree with him for once, even though I suddenly have an urge to go see her.

I bury my face in my arms on the counter.

Maybe I shouldn't have drunk so much.

~

I really shouldn't have drunk so much, I think as I stumble out of the elevator.

Ethan drove me home—well, his driver did—and the doorman downstairs helped me across the lobby, but now I'm on my own and I realize I can barely put one foot in front of the other.

I lean on the wall and trudge along. I can already see the door to my apartment even if it's a bit of a blur.

Just a few more steps...

I fall. One moment I'm leaning on the wall and the next I'm on the floor. I don't feel any pain, though. Just the coarse carpet against my cheek.

And weak. I feel weak. Like I don't think I'll be able to get up.

Fuck.

I close my eyes, about to give up. But then I hear a voice.

"Asher?"

I open my eyes and see Violet kneeling beside me. Just the sight of her alone gives me the strength to get my face off the floor and straighten up half my body so I can sit against the wall. But that's the best I can do.

"Asher?" Violet places her hand on my shoulder. "Are you okay?"

I look into her eyes. Even though I'm drunk, I can see them clearly.

"Beautiful," I mutter.

Her eyebrows crease. "What?"

"You're beautiful," I tell her.

"And you're drunk," she says.

"That doesn't… make it any less true."

She shakes her head.

I narrow my eyes. "Are you blushing?"

"No," she says. "You're the one whose face is all red."

"Do you like it?"

"Just shut up and let me help you get home."

She grabs my arm.

"Wait." I pull it away. "Before I shut up, I have something to say."

I know Ryker said I should wait until I'm sober before I talk to Violet, and he's probably right. But she's here now. I'm not wasting this chance.

Violet looks at me. "Are you sure you don't want to wait until you're sober?"

"No," I answer. "I mean yes. I'm sure."

She sits on her heels. "Okay then. I'm listening. But if you start to speak nonsense…"

"Farrah West," I begin.

Violet crosses her arms over her chest. "Asher, I'm Violet Cleary. I know you're drunk, and I know you're not good with names, but are you seriously telling me you can't remember the name of the last woman you slept with?"

"No, no. Farrah was the first. And the one who broke me. She was fine at first. But when I left her, she accused me of rape. I was sixteen. She was nineteen."

Violet gasps. "What?"

"The charges were dropped. They're not even on my record. And every article about what happened then was wiped out. But I remember what happened. And I learned my lesson—never let a woman get attached to you."

"So that's why you've been sleeping around."

I nod. "I'd sleep with them one night and leave in the morning like you said. But not you. We've had sex a dozen times and I still want you."

"Because the sex is that good?"

"Because it's not just about the sex. Each time I'm with you, everything just feels… right. And I know I'm all wrong for you. I know I say all the wrong things. But I want to be right for you. I can't be perfect. Not right away. Not ever. Because I'm not. And because of that, I can't promise I'll never hurt you or that we'll never fight. But I want to…"

I grip my stomach as I feel it churn.

"Fuck."

"You want to fuck? Now?" Violet rolls her eyes.

"Well, yes," I tell her with a lopsided grin. "But I also want to stay with…"

I stop talking as the churning in my stomach grows more intense. The next thing I know, I'm throwing up on the carpet.

Fuck.

CHAPTER TWENTY-FOUR

Violet

"Fuck." The curse leaves my lips as I see the puddle on the floor.

Well, this is a mess. Then again, I suppose it's only to be expected since Asher is a mess. A drunken mess. And now, a passed out drunken mess.

Great. Just great.

I consider just leaving him to sleep it off in the cold corridor beside his puddle of vomit. But how can I after he just told me all those things, some of which were exactly the words I'd been waiting to hear?

I grab his arm, place it over my shoulder, and try to get him to his feet so I can bring him inside my apartment.

"Come on."

Asher doesn't wake up, but I somehow manage to drag him through the door and into the living room. I try to put him on the couch but fail so I just leave him on the rug.

I remove his vomit-soaked shirt and clean up his face with a damp towel. Then I fetch the duvet from the spare room and cover his body with it to keep him warm.

There. That's better.

His face is still red and he still reeks of alcohol, but at least he doesn't smell like vomit. And he's sleeping soundly now. In the safety and comfort of my living room.

I sit on the couch and shake my head. Unbelievable.

I can't believe he drank so much that he ended up like this. How old does he think he is? Twenty-one? But that's not all I can't believe.

I still can't believe what he said about the first woman he slept with. What a bitch. And I still can't believe he just poured his heart out to me. Yes, he's drunk, but I can tell he meant every word he said.

He wants to be with me.

I reach down to brush some strands of hair off his forehead. Then I stare at his face and smile.

Asher wants to be with me. He finally said it, and now that he has, I just know I want the same thing.

I want to give him another chance. I want to give us both a chance.

Maybe we'll stay together. Maybe we'll fall apart. Who knows? What matters is that we both decide to try.

That's exactly what I'm going to tell Asher tomorrow. But first, I'll have to make sure he remembers what he told me.

I draw a deep breath.

I sure hope he does.

~

"I remember," Asher says as he sits on the couch beside me moments after waking up. "I remember trying to walk down the corridor and then falling. And then you showed up and we talked. I just don't remember how I ended up here."

"That's because you passed out," I tell him. "You threw up and you passed out."

"I threw up?" Asher's eyes grow wide. "In the corridor?"

"Yes."

He glances down. "So that's why I don't have my shirt."

I nod. "That's why you don't have your shirt."

His eyebrows furrow. "Wait. I passed out in the corridor and you brought me in here? By yourself?"

"Yes," I admit proudly.

"Your new boyfriend didn't help?"

"Boyfriend?"

What is he talking about?

"The man who was here in your apartment," Asher explains.

My eyebrows arch. "Oh. You mean Liam?"

"Yes, Liam."

I laugh. He thinks Liam is my new boyfriend?

He gives me a puzzled look. "What's so funny?"

"You making the same mistake I did."

"I have no idea what you're talking about."

"Liam isn't my new boyfriend."

"He isn't?" Asher's eyes grow wide. Then they narrow. "Wait. Is he your house manager?"

"No." I shake my head. "He's an old friend of mine from Zurich. He's a doctor."

"Oh."

"He's here in Chicago because of a patient and he dropped by to see me."

Asher nods. "I see."

He touches his chin as he looks at me.

"So you and Liam aren't in a romantic relationship?"

"No," I answer.

"But he seemed protective of you."

"Really?" My eyebrows furrow. "What did he say?"

"He wanted me to stay away from you."

"Well, that's because I kind of told him about you. Not that I wanted to. He… he just somehow got it out of me."

"So you're close?"

I shrug. "I guess. He's like a brother to me."

"Just a brother?"

I cross my arms over my chest. "Look at you being the jealous one for a change."

"I need to know, Violet," he insists in a serious tone.

Oh. Now he's serious. I guess I need to get serious as well.

I clear my throat. "Liam is just like a brother to me. Nothing more."

"Sure?"

"Sure."

I see the relief on Asher's face. I guess he really was jealous.

"Now, do you remember what you told me last night?" I ask him.

"Some," he answers.

"Like?"

He pauses and scratches the back of his head. "You know what? I think I'll just start over."

"Okay, but you can skip the part about Farrah."

His eyes narrow. "I told you about Farrah?"

"Yes."

"Okay." Asher draws a deep breath. "I've been doing some thinking and I've realized I don't want to let you go. I'm still not sure how to do this, but I want to try and figure it out. And I know you expect a lot of me, so—"

"I don't," I tell him.

He looks confused, so I go on.

"I was expecting too much of you. I know that now. So I'm not going to anymore. I'm not going to rush you and I'm not going to force you to feel things. I'm just going to be here." I hold his hand. "As long as you're here."

"I intend to be." He grips my hand firmly as he looks into my eyes. "Because I'm in love with you, Violet Cleary."

The words take my breath away. My heart stops.

He is? But I thought Stella said he didn't know how to love.

He touches my cheek. "You don't believe me, do you?"

I place my hand over his. "Actually, I do."

And it's true. In spite of all my fears, I believe him with all my heart, which is pounding so hard right now it might just fly out of my chest.

And I feel the same way.

"I love you, too," I tell Asher. "I think I have for a long time."

He smiles as he strokes my cheek. "Then I'm glad we met again."

Me too. Fate may play tricks, but when it brings people together, it sure brings people together.

Asher closes his eyes as he brings his face close to mine. I almost lean forward to meet him halfway, but I remember something. I place my finger over his lips.

He opens his eyes. I see confusion written all over them.

"Is something wrong?" he asks.

"Actually, yes," I tell him.

He still looks confused, so I blurt it out.

"Before we do anything, you need to brush your teeth." I give him a sniff. "And maybe take a shower."

~

I scrub Asher's back as the water trickles down on us. As I do, I notice the tattoo just above his waist. I recognize the symbol.

"You have a tattoo of the symbol for a subset that doesn't belong?" I ask him.

Asher grins over his shoulder. "I knew you'd recognize that."

"But what does it mean?"

He shrugs. "Maybe that I don't want to belong to anyone. But that was before I met you."

He turns to face me. I smile.

"In that case, maybe you need a new tattoo."

"Maybe," he agrees.

Then he just stares at me.

I put my hands on my hips. "What?"

"Can I kiss you now?" he asks, his gaze on my lips.

I hang my sponge back on the peg.

"Sure."

Asher gives me a wide grin. Then he grabs my arms and pulls me even closer to him, close enough that our faces are almost touching. For a moment, he just looks into my eyes as if he's trying to commit them to memory. Then he leans forward and kisses me.

He's kissed me many times before, but this—this is different. This time, as our lips press firmly against each other, I feel like our entire bodies are connected. Our hearts, too. This kiss feels like the beginning of something new.

Because it is.

He deepens the kiss and I respond by kissing him with all the passion I can muster. My hands run over the muscles of his chest. His caress my back and clutch my ass.

"You love my ass, don't you?" I observe out loud.

"I love every bit of you," he answers, but he squeezes my ass just the same.

I chuckle.

"For instance, I love your hair."

He runs his fingers through it.

"Your breasts."

He kisses each one and they grow ripe with heat.

"Your ass."

He squeezes it again and I laugh.

"Your legs."

He runs his hands over them.

"And this."

He presses a kiss on the triangle between my legs. I hold my breath.

Asher pushes me towards the back of the bathtub and makes me sit on the edge. Then he kneels between my legs, lifts them on his shoulders and starts to press his tongue against me. The breath I'm holding leaves me in a gasp.

"Oh God."

He licks the entrance to my most secret part and I start to tremble. His tongue rubs against my sensitive nub and I moan as I grip his hair.

He teases that bud of flesh over and over, each swipe of his tongue sending ripples of pleasure beneath my skin. I throw my head back against the wall. My moans spill and bounce off the bathroom walls.

Somehow, my body is more excited than usual. Maybe it's because of Asher's bold declaration. Maybe it's because I've missed him. Whatever the reason, I can already feel myself teetering over the edge.

"Asher!"

I cry out his name as I fall over. My heels dig into his back. My toes curl. My fingers pull at his hair as wave after wave of pleasure rolls over me.

When it starts to ebb away, I let Asher's hair go but he stays where he is. His tongue enters me and since I just had an orgasm, I shiver. I'm already wet, and yet his tongue gets me even wetter. Hotter.

I'm ready for more.

I push Asher's head away and slide down inside the tub. I go on my knees and lean over the edge. Then I meet Asher's gaze over my shoulder.

"You can fuck me now."

He grins. "With pleasure."

He grips my hips and starts to slide his cock inside me from behind. It rubs against me and lights a fire deep inside my body.

"Mm. Yes!"

He fills me inch by inch. Then he stops. I clutch the edge of the tub and brace myself for the pleasure to come.

It takes me by storm from the very first thrust. With each one, Asher rocks my entire body and fills every nook and cranny of it with heat. My hips come to life and push back against him.

I try to keep up with his pace but when he speeds up, I fail. My head spins. My body trembles.

I push my hips hard against Asher's as pleasure overwhelms me again. My mouth opens wide as all the air flees my lungs. My fingers dig into porcelain.

I'm still trembling when Asher pulls out of me and turns me around. He captures my mouth in a fierce kiss as his hand moves frantically between our bodies. Then I feel his quivering cock against my belly and something warm between my breasts.

Asher breaks the kiss to rest against my shoulder. I feel his warm, rapid breaths against my skin. I wrap my arms around him and wait for him to catch his breath. When he does, he kisses me again. Then he looks into my eyes.

"What are you thinking?" I ask him as I stroke his cheek.

"That I'm lucky to have found you after losing you once."

I smile. "You better not lose me again."

"No. I better not," he agrees.

He takes my hand and kisses it. My heart leaps in my chest.

"Also, I was thinking we should go another round," he says. "In bed."

I see desire flicker anew in his eyes.

"We can," I tell him. "In bed. After breakfast."

"Breakfast?"

"I'm sure you need something in your stomach," I tell him. "Also, I was thinking we could make pancakes together."

In fact, I can think of many things I'd like for us to do together. But let's start with baby steps. Pancakes.

"Or we could see who can make better pancakes," Asher says.

I narrow my eyes at him. "Oh, is that a challenge?"

"Only if you accept it."

And I can think of no reason not to. Life is simply more interesting with challenges, especially when you have someone you love to face them with.

I wrap my arms around Asher's neck and grin. "I accept."

EPILOGUE

Asher

Three months later...

"I win!" I raise my empty glass of eggnog triumphantly.

Beside me, Ethan continues to gulp down his but stops with a quarter to go.

"I give up," he says. "I should never have agreed to a drinking contest with you."

"Oh, come on. Where's your holiday spirit?" I pat him on the shoulder. "Besides, you won't be able to drink so much after the baby comes."

"True," he agrees.

Stella wraps an arm around him. "I think he should stop drinking so much now."

I frown. "Let the guy live a little, Stell. After all, it's almost Christmas."

"Yup." Excitement gleams in her amber eyes. "Eight more days. And three more days before we go to Zurich. Best Christmas present ever."

Ethan touches her cheek. "Well, you deserve it."

"Aww." Stella gives him a kiss.

I turn away to give them some privacy and end up catching Ryker sneaking out of the bar with a blonde.

My eyebrows furrow. I wonder who that is. As for what they're planning on doing, I think I already know.

It looks like Ryker is getting his Christmas present early.

Speaking of early Christmas presents, maybe it's time I give Violet hers.

Now where is she?

Eventually, I find Violet outside the bar, standing just behind the huge Christmas tree in the hotel lobby. She's still on the phone, so I take a moment to admire her in her golden velvet dress. Even now, I still can't believe she's mine.

When Violet sees me, her eyes grow wide. Moments later, she hangs up and slips her phone inside her purse. I walk over to her.

"You're not cheating on me, are you?" I tease her.

"No," she says. "I was talking to my mother."

"Really?"

She nods. "She wants me to come home for Christmas. She wants me to bring you along, too."

"Why not? You haven't been home in a while, right?"

She shrugs. "Well, you know I don't have many fond memories of home."

"I know." I take her hand. "But your mom is all better now, right? Maybe it's time to make some new memories."

Violet says nothing.

I stroke her hand. "Besides, I want to meet her."

Violet's eyebrows arch. "You do?"

I nod. "I want to thank her for bringing such an amazing person into this world."

Violet blushes as she shakes her head. "You don't have to do that."

"And I want to tell her that I'm going to do my best to be a good husband to her daughter."

Violet's eyes grow wide. "What are you talking about?"

I take the satin box out of my pocket and start to go down on one knee. Violet stops me.

"What are you doing?"

"Proposing," I tell her. "At least, that's what I was going to do."

Her eyebrows furrow. "But we've only been together for three months."

"I know. But you also said you've loved me for a long time and that I shouldn't lose you again."

"But—"

I place my finger on her lips. "I can't believe you're arguing with me on this."

"I just…" She swallows. "I don't know if we're ready."

"I know we are," I tell her as I touch her cheek. "You know how I know? Because there's nothing the two of us can't overcome. We're amazing."

Violet says nothing.

I give her a puzzled look. "What? You don't believe that?"

"I do. I know we're amazing. It's just that—"

I silence Violet with a kiss. If there's one thing I've learned these past few months, it's that the best way to stop her from arguing with me is by kissing her. Thoroughly.

After I pull away, I look into her eyes.

"Marry me, Violet."

She gazes back into mine. "You really don't know how to take no for an answer, do you?"

"No."

She chuckles. "Then I guess my answer is yes."

My lips curve into a smile. "Good."

I kiss her again. This time, as I do, I slip the diamond ring onto her finger. She takes a look at it and gasps.

"This is…"

"Real? Yes. Expensive? Yes."

"I was going to say it's incredible," Violet says.

"Just like you." I take her hand and kiss it. "I love you."

Her eyes glisten just like the lights of the tree. "I love you, too."

I never thought I'd find love, but now that I have, I'm never letting it slip through my fingers again.

~*The End*~

If you LOVED Happily Enemy After, be sure to check out Breaking The Bro Code!

It's a fun and flirty hot romance read filled with page melting heat, lots of teasing, drama and some sugar sweet moments guaranteed to leave you with a very satisfying happily-ever-after.

BREAKING THE BRO CODE SNEAK PEEK

I'm a rule follower, always have been,

Nothing says OFF LIMITS like your best friend's little sister,

But the moment my lips touched Claire's,

I threw the whole damn book out the window.

PROLOGUE

Ryker

What's better than being a boy unwrapping your present on Christmas morning? Being a grown man and seeing your Christmas present walk into the room.

She looks just like Christmas in a red tartan dress, sleeveless with a pleated skirt that stops right below her knees and a black ribbon with a shiny golden buckle around her waist. Her blonde hair is braided into a crown, but some tendrils have managed to escape—or were they left out on purpose?—so they now dangle over her cheeks like the tinsel on the tree. Her full lips are bright red like her dress and the rubies attached to her ears. She lifts a hand to rub one of the gems as she says something with furrowed eyebrows. Then her emerald eyes grow wide. They sparkle, more so than any of the lights in the room, as she chuckles. I smile.

Claire Parker. I always thought she'd turn out to be a beauty, even when she was a plump nine-year-old or a teenager stressing over her pimples and her braces and which conditioner to use. But damn, I never imagined she'd be like this supermodel I can barely recognize, this woman who can light up a whole town, who oozes grace and confidence with her every move, who I just can't tear my gaze away from.

When did Claire grow up to be the most attractive woman I've ever set eyes on?

More to come..............

Visit

https://www.ashleepriceromanceauthor.com/

and to find out when Breaking the Bro Code and other Ashlee Price books will be ready in large print.